Goldilocks & The Three Bear Brothers

Second Edition

Overture
Book 3

From the *Naughty Goldie* series

by Pebbles Lacasse

I0671426

Goldilocks & the Three Bear Brothers: Overture

ISBN 978-1-989979-05-1

Cover design © 2020 cover artist Pebbles Lacasse
First Edition April 2021
Photographs by Pebbles Lacasse
Model J M
Published by Pebbles Lacasse
www.pebbleslacasse.com
Edited by: Off the Shelf Editing
https://www.offtheshelfediting.com

CHAPTER ONE

The relationship between the Bear brothers—Patch, Mack, and Bash Bear—has been copacetic.

Mack is neutral and only wants the best for everyone. He loves me, too, but differently than Bash and Patch do. After Patch announced that he's also in love with me, he and Bash fought as if they were real bears fighting over a mate, and I was that mate. It was awful! Eventually, they agreed they can all love me as long as I call Bash's bed my own and dream beside him at night, even if another brother is on the other side of me.

The bruises Patch and Bash sported for a few weeks after their slug-fest was a constant reminder that I was the reason the two came to blows. It was hard to see, even though they had settled their issues. If I didn't love all three brothers so much, I would have walked away so they could restore their bond. But my draw to them is just too strong, and none of them were willing to let me go.

Now that Bash is home from university after graduating with a degree in journalism and English, his job at the *Daily News* takes up a lot of his time. He's been filling in for the regular editor because she's off, having just had a baby.

He's also doing his regular job, which is writing obituaries. Bash believes people deserve to have the very best final sentiments written about them that are deserving of a lifetime. He's sentimental that way, despite his laughing blue eyes that make him look like he doesn't take anything seriously.

When he's not busy at the paper, he works tirelessly on writing his book, which he won't let me read yet. I've tried to sneak up behind him and read over his shoulder, but he always knows I'm there, no matter how quiet I try to be. Once, he continued typing and wrote: *Goldilocks, if you don't go do something with yourself other than hovering over me, I will call Patch over to punish you.*

I was bored and considered testing his threat, but decided I wanted to be able to sit that night without having sore butt cheeks. But sometimes I poke Patch Bear just to provoke him. His aggressive nature is something I crave. He's sure to sexually gratify me after his punishments, and he is damn good at that!

Patch has his crew that helps him cut down trees used for building log cabins and other things; furniture, barns, monuments, et cetera. He also works at the mill when they need extra help. It's physically demanding work, but he loves it. He said there's a satisfaction that comes with creating something beautiful from a chunk of wood. Patch always replaces the trees he's cut down with new sprouts to keep the forest from becoming barren.

Mack, the sweetest yet craziest of the Bear brothers, has been monitoring the build of a three-million-dollar log home he designed. He's quickly becoming one of the most sought-after architects in eastern Canada.

This design is a gorgeous six-bedroom, five-bathroom home that I can't wait to walk through when the build is completed. He said the clients are the owners of a popular fast-food franchise, but I can't remember which one. They own six-hundred acres of land surrounding the lake, making it seem like a private lake. Nobody can own a body of water, but people would have to trespass on their private property, which is illegal. It's going to be a beautiful home when it's completed.

Because the building site is four hours away by car, it isn't feasible for Mack to drive there each day. He stays with some of the construction crew during the week but comes home most weekends, and if the weather is expected to be bad for a few days and they put the build on hold, he'll come home.

He's there more often than he's here. I miss having him around. His brothers miss him, too.

Shaina, Mack's girlfriend, visits Patch now and then for a quick fuck when Mack's out of town. It's allowed because it's never kept hidden as if they're having a secret affair. She hasn't asked to be with Bash, not that we see her much these days. She works a lot, and she's still in college, which keeps her busy.

It's still hard for me to believe that Bash and I have a semi-open relationship. Sometimes I need a minute to sort through my emotions. The brothers always shared everything, including women. They're quite happy knowing I can have sex with any of them whenever I want. The guys are allowed to be with each other's girlfriends, as long as she *and* I allow it.

When I was away at college, Bash had sex with Shaina but didn't tell me right away. I was upset because Mack was the one who told me about it.

Bash hid it from me. In his defense, Bash didn't want to tell me over the phone. This was the first time he'd had sex with another woman besides me since we've been together. He wanted to wait until we were face-to-face, which would have been much better for me.

I've forgiven Bash for not having told me right away, but I think he's afraid to have sex with Shaina again, thinking I might get upset. I won't.

Am I jealous? Perhaps a little; I think it would be abnormal if I wasn't. But I know he'll always come home to me, and I don't worry about him choosing her.

Since I graduated from nursing school and moved back to my hometown, I've been working at the local hospital. Since I didn't have a vehicle of my own, Bash and I had to compare schedules to make sure we got to our destinations on time. I got a loan and picked up a used Dodge Journey, and I love it.

This is the first time I've had my own car and I'm so proud of myself for taking the scary leap into financial debt.

The walls in the log house the guys built for Bash and me seem too stark, so I decided to stop at the second-hand store two towns over to pick up a few pictures to hang. When I bought some furniture here a month ago, I saw some beautiful scenic pictures of mountains and rivers that would be perfect. Hopefully, they're still available.

This store is huge and filled with everything from packaged food to clothing, furniture and pet products. My cart is nearly full of different-sized pictures when a woman walks up to me to introduce herself.

"Hi. Are you Goldilocks?" Her smile reveals crooked teeth.

I'm immediately on defense. "Um, yes."

How the hell does this woman know my name? She doesn't look familiar. Her brunette hair is cropped in a bob. She's short and tiny, aside from her wide hips. She pops her hand out toward me.

"I'm Sarah Joyeau." I take her hand and shake it. She smiles too aggressively for my comfort and then lowers her voice. "Sorry, I know you don't know me. I used to date the Bear brothers a few years ago."

Her hands rest folded together in front of her while she shifts her weight from one leg to the other. What the hell does this woman want?

My heart pounds quicker in my chest. "How do you know who I am?"

She tilts her head. "Everyone knows who you are. You're a hot topic these days." She must see the fear in my eyes and retreats. "No, no! I'm not a crazy person who's going to attack you or anything. I know what you're going through." She steps closer and lowers her voice to a whisper. "People assume you're sleeping with all of them, but they don't know how it really is. I do."

"Oh?" My eyes scan around us, fearing someone might overhear. "And how is it?"

She scratches her head and seems concerned that she's getting herself in too deep. "Um, well, the guys aren't the evil seducers of innocent females like people seem to think. They're really nice guys and wouldn't intentionally hurt a woman, ever!"

"How long ago were you with them?"

Am I prying too deeply? No. She brought it up, so I'm entitled to ask questions. Right?

"A few years ago." She bites her top lip while she looks off in the distance. She suddenly changes the subject. "Do you want help getting these to the front? They're nice pictures. New apartment? Are you decorating?"

I watch as she pulls the frames apart enough to look at each photo. "I think I can handle it. I'm decorating our new house."

She sets the pictures down without looking at the three bottom ones. "Oh, a house? Who are you living with?"

"If you must know, Bash. He's my boyfriend."

Her eyes widen. "Your boyfriend?"

"Is that weird?" I set the framed picture I'm holding back on the pile I've opted not to purchase and give her my full attention.

She waves her hand and then crosses her arms over her chest. "No, not weird. I was dating Mack for a while, but after some time, it seemed like I wasn't dating any one of them in particular. They shared me, often, but I was officially with Mack." Her fingers brush through her hair to pull it off her face, but it slips right back. "Bash was the best lover, and I thought maybe I could let myself love him, too, but he was too closed off. He said his heart belonged to someone else."

"Hmm…" I pause and wonder who the woman was that he loved. "Yeah, Bash and I live together. We don't live in the main Bear residence."

She whispers and speaks quickly. "So, you don't—you know—*play* with Patch and Mack, too? The rumors all suggest that you do, not that I really believe what people say. Well, one woman said she heard that you had sex with them in the forest." She leans close and winks. "I'll admit, I was a teensy bit jealous! I mean, if I could go back and get it on with Bash again…" She forms her lips into an O and widens her eyes, then dances a little shimmy.

"Yeah, well," I clear my throat but don't hide my irritation in my tone. "You're not with them anymore. Since you're being so candid," I pause. "Why did you and Mack break up?"

She pulls her lips in between her crooked teeth and bites down gently while her gaze assesses me. She shrugs and runs her hand through her hair again. That must be a nervous habit.

"Patch sort of scared me." She looks to her left to see if anyone is within earshot. "He's a rough man who has strange kinks. I'm not into rough sex, at least not at his level. I told Mack that I didn't want to be with Patch anymore but still wanted to be with him and Bash. He said either I'm with Patch, too, or none of them. Then I told him that I loved him. He flat out told me he didn't love me and probably never would."

She shrugs and twists her mouth for a second. "He was kind about it, but things were different after that. I had to walk away, but I still miss him and Bash, not so much Patch." She shifts her weight and clasps her hands behind her back. "Do you find Patch to be too rough, or are you into that?"

I cut her off. "Look, what I do with Patch, or don't do, is my business. I don't know you, and I'm not going to discuss my happenings with you."

She seems surprised at my refusal to openly chat with her. "Sorry. I just thought that since we have something in common, we could become friends."

I smile but squint my eyes. "Yeah. I'm not going to start a friendship with you for the sole reason that you had sex with the Bear brothers. If that were the only requirement, I'd have an extensive friends list. Wouldn't I?"

With wide eyes and raised eyebrows, she nods. "Well, if you ever want to talk…" She clears her throat. Again, she runs a hand through her hair, not altering the style whatsoever. "When my friends found out about what I was doing … with the guys … they ostracized me. I had to move out of town to evade the cruelty. I hope that's not the case with you."

She shifts, takes a breath, and turns her attention to the paintings. "Anyway, do you need help with your pictures? I can take them to the front if you want to shop more. If you add one more, they're going to fall out of your cart." She giggles and swings her arms front and back like a child and lifts onto her toes as she does.

"No, I have all I need."

She smiles, turns, and takes a few steps, but I call out to her, not wanting to leave the conversation hanging on my rudeness.

"Hey, um—" I call out. She spins on her heel and takes a step back toward me. "I'm sorry that happened to you. People are cruel. I've had run-ins with judgemental assholes, too."

"You're stronger than me; you're still with them. I couldn't do it."

"The public's bullshit doesn't deter me, and you shouldn't let it bother you either. This is your life; live it how you want to. Fuck those gossiping assholes and their shitty existence." My smirk is met with her laugh.

She nods, laughs again, and quickly scurries away, holding her head a bit higher than she did when she approached me. As she walks away, I picture Patch fucking her while he pulls her hair and spanks her ass. Yeah, I think she's more of a love-maker than a lover of rough sex. I do wish her the best.

CHAPTER TWO

Several sunset pictures fill the empty spaces in my bedroom. Two beach and open field pictures hang in each of the spare bedrooms. Two smaller photos of a lake dangle on nails in the bathroom. I've hung a large mountain view picture in the living room, near the kitchen.

That leaves only one more. It's my favorite; a sunset view from someone's kayak, floating on water that's smooth as glass. The kayak is bright green, a pleasant contradiction from the pink and orange mountains mirrored on the water.

I struggle to hold it up to get a better idea of where to place the nails when a knock on the door startles me and I nearly drop it. I carefully set the heavy frame on the floor.

As I near the door, I spot Patch's truck through the window. My tummy flutters and my pussy clenches. What's he doing here?

"Come on in," I yell.

The door swings open wide and in comes the mountainous man, a wooden bench perched atop his shoulder. He sets it beside the door and bends down to rearrange the shoes and boots to rest beneath it.

It's obvious he made it since it says "Goldie's Bench" along the backrest. The craftsmanship Patch puts into his works never ceases to amaze me. His talent should be featured in a magazine, but he would refuse the opportunity, not wanting to have that much attention drawn his way. He's a quiet man who prefers to stand in silence while assessing everyone in the room. If he wants to be heard, he can easily still a room with his deep voice.

"The seat lifts so you can put stuff inside." He lifts it to show me how it works and then stands tall, admiring the bench. "It looks good there. Don't you think?"

"Yes! Wow! Oh, my G… It's beautiful!" I lift the seat, look inside, then set it down and plop my ass on it while my fingertips caress the decorative backrest. "This is incredible!"

"Thanks, Goldie."

I frown. "We talked about this. I don't like you calling me Goldie. That's Bash's nickname for me, not yours."

His deviant gaze meets my scrunched-up face.

"Like I've told you before, I'll call you whatever the fuck I want." His hands rest on his hips while his brown eyes scream *danger* to me from his 6'3" stance. "Would you have preferred Slut, Whore, or my Little Cunt?"

I lean back on the bench. "Definitely not any of those."

My fingers trace the hand-carved etching of my name. I breathe in the soothing scent of wood and sigh heavily. "Thank you so much. I can't believe you built this for me; built the whole damn house! I mean, I love you guys! You spoil me."

"You deserve to be spoiled." He offers his hand to me. "Come here."

I rise from the bench and step toward him. He gathers me in his thick arms and holds me against his strong chest. His heart beats quickly beneath his khaki t-shirt.

"I love you. I do my best to give you everything…"

His embrace is calm, homey, and familiar as if I've been waiting my whole life to be this happy. My heart thumps evenly with his and it feels right, as it does when I'm with each brother.

"…including my heart," he whispers, then kisses the top of my head.

I smile and pull away from him, finger-brush my hair behind my ear, and return to the picture I sat on the floor.

"What are you up to?" he asks as he follows me around the sofa. I lift the picture, but he's quick to take it from me. "Let me help. Where are you hanging it?"

"Right there." I point to the empty space on the wall. "I think it'll be perfect beside the big window. It's too bare over here. It needs something. I thought about a cabinet but that might make the corner look too crowded."

"You're going to hang it there?" He crosses his arms over his chest and cocks his head.

"That's the plan. It'll look good there." He doesn't look convinced. "You don't think so?" I tilt my head and rethink it.

"No, not here." He draws in a long breath and scans the room. "Over there, beside the door would be better."

I turn to look at the spot. "Definitely not! I doubt it would even fit there." I step toward the spot I chose. "Nope! My mind is made up. I want it here." I gesture with both arms to frame the spot.

He scratches his freshly shaved chin. "Are you sure?"

I press my hand to my throat in frustration and lean my weight on one leg. "Why are you being an ass about this? I told you where I want it." I sigh heavily when he frowns. "I'm quite capable of hanging it myself if you're only going to pout about it. I've hung all the other ones without issue."

His eyes burn into mine. My tummy flutters and my pussy moistens. He finds my defiance arousing and usually punishes me but I like it and test the limits of his patience, often. Right now, I just want the picture hung!

His lips press together and he clears his throat. When his eyes shift to the empty wall, I look down at the bulge in his snug-fitting jeans.

"Fine. Give me the hammer!" He points his finger at me. "And drop the attitude or I'll drop it for you."

My bottom lip pinches between my teeth as I skip away to fetch the hammer and nails from the table. His eyes follow me. I hand the tools to him. His sternness never fails to ignite a flaming desire in my nether region and right now is no different. I'm heating up and my flushed cheeks prove it.

He's so powerful; two bashes and the nail didn't stand a chance. I hit the other ones at least a dozen times to get the same result. He hands me the hammer, then hangs the picture and tilts it to the right to straighten it. He steps back and assesses it before readjusting.

"Do you want a beer?" I ask as I swing the hammer beside my knee.

He leans down and relieves me of the tool. "Careful, little girl. I'd hate to see you whack your knee."

I roll my eyes and spin on my heels to fetch us each a bottle of beer. He follows and sets the hammer on the kitchen table while I lean into the fridge. I hand him a bottle and he spins off the cap with ease, while I grip mine and struggle. He hands me the open one and takes mine. He spins off the cap before he tips the bottle to swallow half of it in one gulp.

I take the caps from him and toss them while I offer him a seat at the table, to which he accepts.

"How's the job at the hospital going?" he asks.

I sit across from him and rest my feet on the chair next to me, and then take a long gulp. "The job itself is great, and most of my coworkers are nice. But there are a few that treat me like—" I roll my eyes and sip the beer. "Well, I'd be happier than a pig in a mud puddle if I never had to see them again."

"People can be assholes," he adds.

"It's not only my coworkers," I mumble.

"What's going on?" He leans toward me and rests his elbows on the table while he clutches the nearly empty beer bottle.

I tug at my earlobe. "Nothing you need to concern yourself with."

Seeming annoyed, he hisses, "Talk to me, Goldie."

I scowl at his use of the nickname. "I was told that most people know—or think they know—about my intimate relationship with all three sexually abusive Bear brothers."

He chuckles. "And that bothers you."

I shrug my shoulders but don't meet his gaze. Instead, I look at my beer label with a slight satisfaction that I got it off without tearing it. He doesn't need to know about the woman at the store or the judgemental general public who glares at me as I go about my life.

"Some of my coworkers give me a hard time." I sip from my bottle. "It's hard to tell if they're appalled or jealous. Either way, they treat me like shit whenever they can. There isn't a lot I can do about it since they have seniority." I soften my voice to seem more innocent. "I simply smile and bat my eyelashes."

"What do they do when you do that?"

I undo the ponytail from my hair and shake out my tresses. "They either pity me or glare and storm off. I think my lifestyle bothers them more than their attitude about it bothers me. I really don't care what people think. I have friends at the hospital who don't judge me, and I appreciate them. The others can go fuck themselves and probably do because who'd want to fuck a miserable bitch that's always complaining?"

He snickers and rubs his chin. "I'd grab that bitch by the hair, kiss her mouth hard, force her over a table, and fuck the hell out of her until she passed out from coming too hard. That might get her to loosen."

I lick my lips and savor the thought. "Oh?" I sip my beer, drop my feet to the floor and square my shoulders. "Well, that always loosens me up." My expression screams naughty intention.

He leans back in his chair and rests his hand on the bulge in his jeans as he sucks back the last gulp of beer. "Careful, Goldie. I'm in a mood."

I lean back in my chair and ape his position while I slug my beer until it's empty. I stifle a burp and set the bottle on the table. His gaze is locked on the hand that rests on the crotch of my dark grey yoga pants.

"And what kind of mood are you in, exactly?" I sink my hand deeper between my thighs. I don't touch my pussy but it's close enough.

He tilts his head forward and looks at me from under his brows. I'd swear his dark brown eyes turn black and sink a little deeper in his skull.

Patch rises and rounds the table while my eyes follow. My tummy flutters like a hundred bees are buzzing. He offers his hand to me and I set my much smaller hand across his giant palm.

He yanks and quickly pulls me to my feet. He hugs me to his body and lifts me off my feet. As if I'm weightless, he carries me effortlessly to the island while he kisses me. His hot tongue fills my mouth and I suck on it to arouse him further. He groans against my lips.

He spins me as he sets me on my feet but leaves his hand spanned across my shoulder blades. He presses my upper body on the countertop while his fingers reach under my shirt to hook the waistband of my yoga pants. He yanks them down to bare my ass.

"No panties." He groans his approval. "Good girl."

His massive hand glides down my back and rests on my bare ass, covering both cheeks. He weaves the other into my hair and turns my head until my cheek rests on the counter.

"Grip the other side of the counter and hang on." As I do, his voice deepens. "Don't let go."

I know better than to assume his order to be a mere suggestion. I reach up and stretch my torso over the island and grip the opposite edge.

He caresses my ass one cheek at a time. He squeezes my left buttock until I whimper and then cracks me hard with his open palm.

Fuck! That hurts!

"Your punishment is ten spanks for giving me an attitude about where to hang the picture." He caresses the sensitive, welting skin. "Don't make a sound and I'll reward you. What's your safe word?"

With a shaky voice, I reply, "Red."

He cracks me again and again until he's satisfied ten are enough. My ass is hot and tears have dripped onto the counter, but I was strong and didn't scream.

Patch stands me up when he sees my flushed, tear-soaked face. He doesn't like to see me cry so he wipes away my tears with compassion. Satisfied that no more fall, he grips my hair and pushes me onto the counter. I grip the opposite edge.

He stands behind me and kicks my feet apart until he can stand between them. My pelvic bones hold my weight painfully on the counter's edge, but I don't care to complain because I kind of like it. His fingers glide between my ass cheeks, over my asshole, and between my drenched pussy lips before delving deep into me. I wiggle, jutting my ass toward him as a plea for more. He pulls his fingers out but slips them further down between my lips until he reaches my clitoris.

I moan as his fingers tenderly rub tiny circles over my stiff button. His hand raises and he whacks my ass once more, jolting my thoughts away from my clit and back to the pain of my red-hot ass.

"I said to be quiet, didn't I?" He whispers as his fingers find my clit to continue their delicious assault. "I don't want you to make a sound until I tell you to cum. Do you understand?"

Knowing better, I say nothing; he told me not to make a sound. From past experience, to verbalize my understanding is cause for more swats. I simply nod the best I can despite my hair held in his vice-like grip. It isn't painful as much as immobilizing.

Patch pushes his fat thumb into my pussy. I tighten when he circles my clit. I try to remain calm and not cum but I'm so close, and he knows it. He won't stop until he's satisfied I obeyed his order and refused myself an orgasm.

He moves his hand and quickly fills me full of his thick, hard cock. My walls stretch and then clench as soon as he's buried deep. My breath escapes me. He holds still until I breathe.

"Don't let go of the counter, and don't lift your head."

He frees my hair and a matted wad quickly drapes over my face. I try to blow it away from my eyes but it doesn't move.

"I'm going to fuck you hard and fast; how you like. Not a sound. Don't cum until I permit it."

His pelvis rests against my ass as his hands slide along my skin and settle on my waist. He pulls back and makes good on his promise. He pounds into me. My fingertips barely hold the counter and my hip bones grate on the counter's edge.

Oh, fuck! I want to cum! It's right there. If I just let go, I'll cum so hard. Somehow, I manage to withhold the moans. At some point, I think I blackout but I can't be sure.

Oh, my God! Please let me cum!

He grabs my forearms and hisses, "Let go." When I do, he pulls them behind my back and holds my wrists tightly in one hand while his other presses on my lower back to pin me to the counter. He rams; hard, fast, incredibly fast.

"Tell me you're my slut!" he demands.

"I'm your slut!" I scream.

"My slut! My dirty little fucking slut." He slams a few more times and my pussy tightens around his cock. "Cum, whore! Fucking cum!"

A slow, steadily increasing scream builds as I let myself fall into the muscle clenching, mind-blowing euphoria of my climax. I hear him spit words at me but I have no idea what he's saying, and I don't care. My thoughts have sunk into blackness while my body floats high above the counter. I never want this to stop.

Patch wails, slams into me three more times, and then stiffens. His cock swells inside me and stretches my spasming pussy as it chokes him, desperate to keep the pulsing shaft wedged deep into me.

I'm exhausted, yet my mind is ripe with energy.

Patch's withered cock slips from me and we both groan. He releases my wrists, then grasps my hips to ensure my feet are firmly on the floor. He wraps his heavy arms over my shoulders and holds my back against his burly chest while I catch my breath.

Between breaths, he asks, "What am I going to do when you're not mine anymore; when you decide you only want Bash?"

"What do you mean? I'll always want you." I turn to look at his flushed face.

"There will come a day when you won't. When you and Bash decide to start a family, continuing what we have won't be feasible, and you know it." He sighs, then kisses my head. His eyes scan my body. "If you were mine—"

I snap at him. "You should keep in mind that I will never be yours. Bash allows us to love each other, and I'll allow you my body whenever you want, but he comes before you or Mack." I step back and look into his stoic face. "Please, don't suggest I be only yours."

"No, that's not what I was…" He groans frustratedly. "You're making a thing out of nothing. I was just saying that if you were mine—"

I raise my hand and shake my head to beg him not to continue. He holds up his hand to stop me from saying what he knows I'm about to.

He raises his voice. "Just hang on a minute, woman! Since you went there … you know I love you. We all agreed it's okay that we love each other." He leans his back against the counter and calms his voice. "You will want something different in the future. I wasn't suggesting I was going to take you away from Bash. I was just—"

I cut him off. "You couldn't if you tried." I yank my pants up and wiggle my hips until the material slips into place.

Calmly, despite his flared nostrils, he asks, "Where is this coming from?"

I stop fussing with my pants to meet his eyes. "You said *if you were mine…*"

"Holy fuck, woman!" He groans and slaps his forehead. "Can't a man say something to you without you blowing it into something it's not? I wasn't suggesting I wanted you for myself. I was about to say that I'd never let you wear clothes if you were mine. But since you took this conversation in that direction…"

My shoulders sag. I feel like an idiot. "Well, I'm not yours," I insist. Before I can walk away, he has me by my arm. I freeze but don't turn to look at him.

"Don't walk away from me angry." His words are loud and stern. "Never walk away from me angry!"

I slowly turn my head to look at the fist wrapped tightly around my bicep. With my head tilted forward, I raise my eyes to meet his. "You'd be wise to let me go."

"Promise you won't walk away. We need to resolve this."

When my gaze falls back to the hold he has on me, he releases his grip and puts his hands in the air to surrender. I slowly walk to the fridge and lean against it with my arms crossed over my chest, and sport pursed lips.

He steps back and resumes his spot against the counter and rests the heels of his hands on the edge.

Perhaps I misunderstood him. I ask, "What did you mean when you said that thing about me not being yours anymore? When was I ever yours?"

He shakes his head and walks toward me, places his hands on my shoulders, and urges me to move aside. When I do, he opens the fridge and takes out two beers. He opens one and hands it to me, then opens the other and tosses the bent caps in the trash. We take long sips as he makes his way to the table and sits in the chair he sat in before we fucked. I take his lead and sit and attempt to peel this label too but sadly, it tears.

He slugs down a gulp from his bottle. "Every second I'm inside you, you belong to me. You're mine, and I'm yours."

I sip my beer.

He continues. "It's no secret I love you. Bash and Mack love you, too. Each of us loves you differently. When a man's inside you, at that moment, you belong to him. We all know Bash owns your heart, and if you had to choose, you'll always choose him. Nobody wants that to change. But in the moments when you do belong to us, it's nice to pretend." His gaze doesn't meet mine.

"Well, don't I look stupid?" I look down at the table and spread out the torn label. I run my fingers over it to flatten it out.

His voice softens. "You're not stupid. You simply didn't know how it is for us." He puts the bottle to his lips and tilts it until he's sucked back every drop. His eyes finally meet mine. "Well, I should get back to work. I'm sure the crew is slacking off since I'm not there to light a fire under their asses."

"Your people are excellent employees. They'll get the job done whether you're there spitting out orders or not."

He raises his brows and nods. "I know, but I should get going."

I rise and circle the table, and then flop my ass on his lap and wrap my arms around his head. "Let me assure you that I'm not considering having children any time soon. I'm sorry I flipped out. I don't know why I did that."

"Female hormones!" he says without hesitation, and I let out a harsh breath in protest. "Take it easy. Men will never understand how female hormones work, and women can't control them to no fault of their own." He laughs, then places a long kiss on my forehead. "Thanks for the memorable afternoon. Is your ass okay?"

I scoff. "Tough guy, you'd have to hit me harder than that to break me down." I run my fingers through his army-style haircut. "I belong to Bash first but I also belong to you and

Mack. I'm a spoiled woman; loved by three sexy, hunky men."

"I would move Heaven and Earth for you; bring you the moon and the stars."

I cup his face in my palms and press my forehead against his. "I would never ask you to do something that extreme." I kiss his nose. "But having my very own star would be freaking awesome! Then again, I'm not sure where I'd keep it."

He lifts me to my feet as he rises. "I'll work on that."

He places one finger under my chin and lifts my face so he can plant a loving kiss on my lips. He rushes off and leaves me feeling lonely.

CHAPTER THREE

I put the tools back in Bash's toolbox, then take a shower. Just as I'm leaving the bathroom, I hear my phone singing in the kitchen. My feet slap on the floor as I run down the hall. I turn the corner and *BAM*!

My feet slide out from beneath me and I thud to the floor. I'm sprawled out and shocked by my clumsiness but sigh with relief that I don't immediately feel any critical pain. I crawl my way to the counter. I reach up but the ringing has stopped.

I tap Bash's name and press the phone to my ear as I lean back against the cabinet. As it rings, I assess the red mark on my forearm that will surely worsen. I rub it and that seems to help.

"Hi, Goldie." I can tell he's smiling just by his tone. "What have you been up to?"

"Hi," I reply. "Patch came over and fucked the hell out of me so I had to take another shower. As I was getting out, I heard my phone ring in the kitchen. Well, I met the floor on my race to answer." I laugh.

He chuckles while he asks, "Are you hurt?"

"No, not really." I glance at my arm. "Just a bruise."

"Did you at least enjoy your time with Patch?" he asks.

"I did," I reply with a softness in my voice. We should consider putting rubber bumpers around the edge of the island. My hip bones are bruised."

He laughs. "So, do you want me to put rubber bumpers on all the counters or just the island?"

"Maybe we can get Patch to limit his play radius to the island to save on the cost of rubber." I stand and get the ice bag from the freezer and mold it around my forearm, then sit on an island stool. "So, what's up?"

"What else are you up to?" he asks.

I debate. "I was going to paint the trim on the old mirror I bought for our bedroom. Other than that, clean and catch up on the laundry."

"I ran a load through the washer but forgot to run it through the dryer." He clears his throat and says something but the phone isn't near his mouth. He returns. "Sorry, Goldie. That was my boss. I was hoping to be done so I could help Patch down some dead trees to stock for firewood but I'm going to be here for a few more hours."

He shuffles some papers and then says something away from the phone. He sighs and says, "I'm calling to suggest that I pick up some Chinese food on my way home. We can invite Patch and Mack, too—have a family night. What do you think?"

"Me, not cooking? You won't hear me complain." I celebrate with a body wiggle. "I'll text the guys to ask if they can make it. I'll ask Mack if Shaina can join us."

"Sounds great. Just text me the headcount." He pauses. "Babe, I have to let you go."

"Okay, don't work too hard."

"I'm sitting at a desk. This is not hard work. Keeping up with Patch while he downs trees is hard work," he chuckles. "Okay, text me later. Love you!"

"I love you," I say but I think he hung up too quickly to have heard it.

After I send texts to both Mack and Patch, I slip on a loose-fitting knee-length dress, put my hair in a ponytail, and start speed cleaning.

***

The guys and Shaina should all be here in fifteen minutes. I could set my clock to the brothers. They're always on time. I don't know how they do it. I can plan with plenty of time to spare but somehow I still manage to be late.

I open the door and step aside. Bash has his hands full of food bags and his satchel hangs by his elbow and it looks heavy. He jogs through the downpouring rain while he tries to keep the food bags dry.

He rushes in and kisses me as he kicks off his shoes and kicks them under the bench. I take two of the bags and set them on the dining room table that I already pre-set. He sets his satchel on the bench, then grabs me and nestles me in his arms.

"How much time do we have?" He lifts his wrist to check his watch.

"Not enough time for what you're thinking." I wiggle from his clutches.

He pouts while his arms raise at his sides. "I can be fast!" His come-hither grin has me debating whether to lift my skirt or not. "Better yet, I bet I can get you off before they arrive."

I glance at the kitchen clock shaped like an apple. "We don't have time. They'll be here any minute." I open the sturdy paper bags and take out the cardboard containers. The smell fills my nostrils and my mouth waters. "What has you so excited?"

His eyes narrow and he pours himself a glass of water. "I kept picturing you getting fucked against this counter." He taps the island and takes a long drink, nearly emptying the glass.

"If only I had taken pictures." My eyes scan his body. "I suppose your imagination will have to suffice."

"After they leave, I'm going to make you cum on my face," he promises as he lifts my chin. "I love you, Goldie."

I whisper, "You'd better!"

Three heavy-handed knocks interrupt our moment. The solid, hand-carved door swings open. Shaina enters first; Mack and Patch follow.

Shaina leans toward me with her bright red lips and feigns a kiss on my cheek, then hands me a bottle of red wine. "Here you go, doll." She kisses Bash and wipes the lipstick from his lips. "Goldilocks, crack that shit so we can get this party going."

Bash seems unaffected by her suggestive touch but their gaze lingers. He offers to take the bottle when he notices I've been studying their silent communication.

Mack wraps his thick arms around me and tilts me back quickly. My screech quickly turns to laughter. I'm safely held in his arms. He plants a long kiss on my lips.

Patch's deep voice rings out. "Hey! Share the love, brother."

"Your lips are sweet as honey." Mack lifts me upright and hands me off to Patch. I'm still grinning from the way Mack swung me with such ease like I weigh nothing.

"It's good seeing you again," Patch says while he grins flirtatiously.

He scans my body, then his hand glides up my back and his fingers weave into my hair. He grips a wad and jerks my head to assert his dominance—like there was ever any question. My pussy clenches. He loves to be in control. When he does things like this, it turns me on as quickly as flipping on a light switch. He snickers when my lower lip quivers.

"Did you miss me?" he whispers seductively brushing his lips against mine, teasingly. I whimper and he pulls his lips away. "You fucking want more, don't you? You're an insatiable little whore." One side of his mouth lifts and he winks playfully.

My nipples are hard as marbles and my panties are damp. "Yes, but I'm *your* whore."

"If you two are done, we can sit and eat," Bash says as he walks past us with the salt and pepper in hand. "You can continue this later for the after-dinner entertainment, but right now, I'm famished. Let's do some power eating."

Patch releases my hair. I run my fingers through it to release any knots that may have formed. I'm still a little frazzled when I sit beside Bash.

He leans toward me so I lean in. He runs the back of his finger down my cheek. "You're so fucking horny right now. Aren't you?"

I swallow while my cheeks flush and a smile lights up my face. "Most definitely!"

He smirks. "Are you rethinking your decision not to let me make you cum before they arrived?"

I bite my lip and reach for the closest cardboard box, hoping it'll take my mind off my pussy's yearn for either mouth or cock.

We chit-chat and talk about what each of us did today. I love how our conversations always lead to a funny childhood story. At one point, I almost choke on a bite of General Tao Chicken because I laugh so hard.

We're stuffed but still manage to eat fortune cookies. Bash takes the conversation in a different direction. "I asked you all here so we can discuss our relationships." Everyone's attention turns to him. "We all know everyone has access to Goldie, which makes her very happy, so in turn, makes me happy. Shaina is also available to everyone, I assume."

She nods with enthusiasm.

I interrupt. "Where is this going?"

He takes my hand and continues. "Patch, you're in love with Goldie, and I'm okay with that, as you know. She has a big heart and has room for all of us. You agreed that hers and my relationship will always come first and I appreciate that, but…"

Patch glances my way. I frown and shake my head because I have no idea what he's about to say. Patch leans back in his chair and exhales heavily. His fear of losing me may be a sentence away. A muscle in his jaw twitches and his eyes drop to the tiny paper that suggests his fortune.

Bash looks at Patch. "Well, you're madly in love with her. It can't be denied. You know I love you, brother…" He pauses to examine the anticipation on everyone's faces and ends with Patch's questioning eyes. "I can't think of anyone I'd rather share my Goldie's heart with than you…" He pauses again and jokes, "Other than Mack, of course. He's a far better human than you, but his heart belongs to Shaina."

Patch takes a loud breath, then clears his throat before he looks at Mack and agrees. "A far better human indeed."

Shaina gloats and hugs Mack's arm. He leans in and pecks her forehead. She looks at me and smiles, so I return the gesture but my smile isn't aimed at her relationship with Mack; I'm more excited to know what Bash will say next.

Patch's scratchy voice breaks through the pause. "What are you getting at, brother?" He sits up and leans his elbows on the table while he folds the tiny paper.

"A proposal." Bash also leans his elbows on the table but weaves his fingers together. "Patch, move in with us. It doesn't have to be full-time. That's up to you. We can give it a try and see how it goes."

Bash and I have talked about Patch moving in but the conversations were fleeting and I didn't think he was serious. Of course, I would love to have Patch here with us.

Bash adds, "We'll have to work out the fine details like where you're going to sleep, for instance. The guest room is an option. Goldie has to be beside me at night. I don't care if you're in the bed with us but she *dreams* beside me. We can work through any issues as we come to them."

Patch's perpetually pissed-off-at-the-world expression eases into a rarely witnessed toothy smile. He stands and Bash follows his lead. They meet and embrace with slaps on the back as men often do when they hug.

Patch beams. "I love you, brother. Thank you."

Bash replies. "I love you, too, big galoot."

Shaina, in her overzealous way, asks, "Well, Goldilocks? What do you say? Do you want Patch to move in? You know he's going to fuck you raw every chance he gets." She turns back to Mack with raised eyebrows. "That boy likes to fuck hard!"

Mack agrees.

Patch and Bash separate and look at me as if anticipating whether I'm okay with this or not. Expressionless, I look at Shaina, then Mack, who lifts his eyebrows to suggest I answer. When I look at Bash, his grin beams; he knows I'm all in. Patch, on the other hand, has never looked so vulnerable. Does he fear rejection? Would it crush him if I said no?

"Yes!" I stand, and they hug me and pin me between them with Patch facing me. "Of course, I want you here."

Shaina interrupts. "So, does that mean you're distancing yourself from Mack? I mean, if you're too exhausted with these two sexual beasts pawing at you all the time, you aren't going to have any energy left for Mack."

I turn my face but Patch's arm blocks me from meeting her eyes. "I'm sure I'll find some energy at some point..." I wiggle to get free so I can look at the two still seated at the table. "If I can ever get away from these two long enough. Don't worry, Mack, I'm not going to disown you."

Mack grins. "You'd better not forget about me! But I'm not worried. I know you'll miss having my cock in your ass."

I feel my face blush. Patch takes my hand and leads me out the front door.

"What are you doing? It's raining!" I complain.

He picks me up wedding style and carries me back through the doorway, setting me down. "I was just making it official."

Mack says, "That's how a groom carries his bride over the threshold, dumbass!"

The two men glare at each other and then laugh.

Shaina asks, "What happens if Patch finds a woman he wants to date? Is he still going to live here?"

"If he wants to," I say with a shrug. "If it comes up, he can decide then."

Patch takes his seat at the table and looks at Shaina. "I might distance myself so I can get to know her to see if it's a sure thing or not. If it becomes something more substantial, we'll sit down and vote whether she can join us as one big happy fucking family, literally."

I feel my heart sink. "If you fall in love with someone else and she refuses to join our big happy fucking family, will that be it for you and me?"

Patch bites his lip, looks down at the tiny folded paper, and tips his head to the side. "Why don't we cross that bridge if it ever comes up."

Bash calmly says, "That sounds fair. We wouldn't expect you not to be with someone else if it's what you want to do."

Mack shoots his arm in the air like a child in a classroom. "I have a question." Everyone looks at him. "What about kids? Who is going to impregnate Goldilocks when the time comes that she wants to pop out a few tiny screaming humans?"

"Wait a minute!" My arm waves at Mack. My lungs feel overly filled with excruciatingly hot air. "What if I don't want kids?"

The room falls silent. Bash looks at me and squints. "She'll have my baby first if it's what she desires."

Patch asks me, "You don't want kids?"

I shrug and laugh. "I'm twenty-three years old and nowhere near ready for shitty diapers, baby screams throughout the night, or teething." My heart pounds hard at the thought of all that responsibility.

Shaina puts her hand on mine. "Goldilocks, you'd have lots of help. It's not like you'd be doing it alone." Her kind words don't help my heart to slow to a more acceptable beat.

Bash rubs his hand on my back. "If you don't want to have children, that's okay with me. I would love to hear the sounds of children's laughs echoing off these walls but it's not a deal changer if it's not your dream, too."

"I—I do want kids *one day*. Not now! But one day." I swallow. "Maybe in about five years."

Patch stands and walks to the kitchen and collects six beers from the fridge. He walks around the table and offers each of us a bottle. Shaina seems annoyed that we have chosen to drink beer but haven't finished our glasses of wine. I didn't care for the taste but I'll empty my glass to be polite. Of course, I'll chase it with beer.

Patch remains standing at his spot at the table and holds up his beer. "To a future built on love and understanding."

Everyone clinks bottles before they shout, "Cheers!" then swig from their bottles.

The thought hits me: where the hell am I going to find the energy to keep up with two sexually charged men?

After everyone has left, I fill the sink with water and slip the plates in. Bash cleans the table, then wraps his arms around my shoulders. He kisses the top of my head and rests his cheek on it.

"Goldie, I love you so much. Are you sure you're on board with Patch living here?"

I attempt to turn but wait for him to loosen his hug. "Yes, I want him here. I love both of you so much."

He kisses me softly, scoops me in his arms, and lays me out on the island. He grabs my calf and uses it to turn me into position. He stands between my dangling calves and locks eyes with me. He slowly lifts my skirt up my thighs.

"No panties?" He watches his thumb caress my smooth pussy lips. "I like that." I giggle. "What's so funny?"

"They were damp so I took them off after dinner," I reply, then snicker. "You and Patch are so similar it's scary." He shakes his head not understanding why I think that. "I wasn't wearing panties this afternoon and Patch reacted the same way you did."

"Well, we are brothers." He smiles but it fades when his thumb delves deeper between my folds.

He slides a stool under his butt and sits. He lifts my legs and places them over his shoulders and rests his elbows on the counter. He reaches over my tummy and weaves his fingers together, essentially holding me in place. He leans in and pecks his puffy lips to each pussy lip, then glides his tongue to where his thumb was. He licks, sucks, and flicks until I've screamed through a powerful orgasm.

Bash scoops me up and takes me to the bedroom, strips me, and tucks me into bed. He undresses and slides in behind me. He didn't ask for his pleasure; his desire was my pleasure. Sleep comes quickly.

CHAPTER FOUR

My workday felt like one of the longest days of my life. The last thing I wanted to do was cook dinner. When Mack called to suggest we meet for pizza at Fazio's Restaurant, I had mixed emotions.

We've never gone out in public together—all four of us—and I'm worried people will stare or worse, say something rude about our relationship. Most of the townsfolk have made it absolutely clear they don't approve. There are a handful of people who accept us. I wish everyone did.

Patch is already at the restaurant and seated when we arrive. This is our first family dinner in a public restaurant since our secret lifestyle hit the rumor mill and spread like wildfire. I didn't want to go but the guys insisted we stop hiding and get back to living among the masses.

As I approach the table with Mack and Bash in tow, Patch stands and pulls a chair out for me. Before I sit, he pecks a kiss on my lips.

Gasps and hushed voices fill the room. Patch's eyelids flutter and a muscle in his jaw clenches but he smiles despite them. I sit while he scans the diners for anyone staring at us. Nobody meets his eyes. He sits as do Bash and Mack who seem unaffected by the whispers followed by glances from entire tables of people.

Patch already ordered for us since he knows what we all like on our pizza and that we enjoy beer. As soon as we're seated, Bash reaches for my hand and holds it. I stare at how long his fingers are. They make my hand look so tiny and delicate.

"Are you okay?" Bash draws my attention. His head tips toward me with concern in his eyes.

"My hand looks childlike next to yours." I brush my hair behind my ear and smile while he assesses our hands.

"You do have puny hands," he snickers.

The waitress sets our bottles in front of us and disappears into the kitchen. When I look around the table at each guy, they look happy and oblivious to the whispers that contain my name and occasionally theirs. I know they can hear it but they choose to ignore it.

I don't want to be talked about. I suppose I lied to Sarah when I said I don't let other people's judgments affect me. I have to get out of here.

"Excuse me." I stand and tuck my purse under my arm. It's hard not to run when the stares follow me as I pass each table. I shove the women's washroom door open and rush inside. The moment the door closes, I take a deep breath and hold it. Slowly, I let it seep out while I look at myself in the mirror, silently giving myself courage.

A woman and small child come out of a stall. The mother is smiling until she sees me standing at the counter. She holds the child up so she can wash her hands. Her eyes dart to me when I run my fingers through my hair so I don't look like an idiot just standing in the women's washroom. She sets her down and hands her a paper towel, then turns to wash her own hands.

"Hi," the little girl bounces as she dries her hands. Her yellow dress swings and she touches mine. "You're wearing a dress, too. Mine's yellow and it's shorter than yours but I like it."

The mother hisses, "Shirley, don't bother the lady."

"She's no bother," I say while I smile at the curly-haired tot. "Your dress is much prettier than mine," I pause, "and those shoes are fancy too."

She smiles and tap dances her shiny shoes while she watches her feet. I look up at the mom and she's glaring at me. My smile falls away and I tilt my head and brush my hair behind my ear.

"Let's go, Shirley. It's very dirty in here." She guides the tot by her shoulders and pulls the door open. With another disgusted leer at me, she walks out.

I swallow hard, then wash my hands and splash some cool water on my face. A tall, heavyset woman walks in and stops walking toward the stalls when she sees me dabbing my face with a paper towel.

"Hey, listen," she says as she nears me. "People are assholes who seem to need something to humiliate to make themselves feel good about their shitty lives." She puts her hand on my shoulder. "Before you walked in, they were whispering about how fat I've gotten this year."

I grimace. "People are assholes. I'm sorry they do that to you."

"No worries," she says with a smile. "I don't let it bother me. My thyroid went haywire and then my MS flared up. I've been riding a recliner for a while now." She laughs. "But I'm here. I'm alive, and I'm still smiling."

She takes a few steps closer. "You're a smart, grown-ass woman who can make her own life decisions. You love them and it's obvious how much they adore you, so don't let other people drag you down. This is your life, live it your way. Now let me give you a hug; you look like you can use one."

I turn and she wraps her arms around me and sways slightly. Her softness and warmth comfort me. She steps back and smiles. "There, now go live your best life and don't let the shallow-minded people bring you down."

She goes into a stall and I resume staring at myself in the mirror. I dab the water off my forehead, then clench my jaw. "You're right," I say to the woman who's now peeing. As I walk out, I call back to her, "Thank you!"

With my head held higher, I walk with purpose to three men that are pleased I've returned.

Patch leans toward me and whispers. "Are you okay?"

My smile is one-sided and I tilt my head. "I'm great, actually."

He twirls a lock of my hair as he memorizes my face. The waitress interrupts when she places a king-sized pizza in the center of the table after moving the condiments caddy.

We eat and laugh as families do. I take my cues from the guys and ignore any whispers of my name or stares meant to intimidate us. It's a much better dining experience than I thought it would be. Before we leave, I smile at the lovely woman from the washroom who showed me how to be courageous. She returns my smile, then waves. I wave, then allow Bash to usher me outside.

Mack and Patch drive back to the main house, and Bash and I go to our house.

He shuts down the engine and the headlights flick off. It's very dark but the tease of moonlight peeking around the treetops brushes Bash's face. His eyes shadow and he looks different; scarier and larger somehow.

The serenade of cicada's resume their screams and the night birds screech as they zip through the evening sky. A light breeze has the trees weaving in a slow dance. Through the clearing, tiny white caps brighten the river as it rushes over the rocks.

The back of his fingers caress down my cheek and my heart flutters. The orchestra fades into the background. He looks at me as if this is the first time he's seeing my face. He tucks a loose tuft of hair behind my ear and then kisses me with the softness of a kitten's fur.

"I'm going to make love to you tonight," he whispers.

My chest feels full. I kiss him more vigorously and put my knee on my seat. I lift my skirt and pull my panties off while he fusses with his belt, button, and zipper, and then lifts his ass to pull his jeans down to mid-thigh.

Neither of us wants to wait until we get in the house.

He wraps his hand around the back of my head and pulls my lips to his. I fling my leg over his lap and brace my shin on the door's armrest. I seem to have way more skirt than I thought, and both of us wrestle with it. I laugh and soon he laughs, too. Our lips part so I can jostle my legs while he pulls the skirt from between us.

I lift and he guides his rock-hard shaft between my slick folds. We moan against each other's lips as I slowly envelop him.

His eyes bear proof of his love for me. I lift and lower unhurriedly so I can savor every invading inch of him. I breathe in his breath—his soul—and give myself to him.

"I love you," I whisper. My pussy feels fuller as though his cock swells.

Bash moans on my lips. "You're my world, Goldie. You have my heart." I increase my pace and he moans again. "I love you so fucking much!"

His arms wrap around my back and pull me against him. He tries to hold me still but I glide my hips back and forth and press my lips just beneath his ear. It must be the hot button spot because his head tips back against the seat.

"Goldie…" He moans and holds me tighter. "Stop. Not yet. Please." He's desperate to regain control but I continue to rock my hips. "Oh, fuck!" He groans. "Don't stop! Don't stop!"

His body tenses and his arms squeeze tighter. His face contorts as if in pain as he loses himself in a powerful climax. His cock swells inside me. I savor every jerk of his muscles and twitch of his cock. I watch his expression slowly ease as he comes back to me with a long, emptying groan.

My forehead rests against his. He swallows between ragged breaths. His arms have eased their grip, but he hasn't released me. I wrap my arms around his neck.

I'll never forget his whisper in the dark. "Don't ever let go."

"Never," I reply without a voice, but he hears me nonetheless.

I have yet to free his spent penis but it's time; my knees ache. After a gentle kiss, I flop onto the passenger's seat.

He whispers, "We should go in."

I reply, "We should have a bath."

"That sounds amazing." His eyebrows raise and he grabs the door handle. "Last one in is a rotten egg!"

He flings open his door, hops out, and nearly trips when his pants drop to his calves. I whip open my door and hit the ground running. I'm halfway to the house and he's catching up quickly.

Just as I leap for the steps, he grabs my waist and yanks me back, then gently shoves me away from the porch. He leaps up the steps three at a time. He fights with his key and opens the door just as I grab hold of his shirt.

I'm laughing so hard I can barely move, let alone run. He steps into the house and turns, twisting his shirt around his waist. He trips over the bench Patch made and falls onto the seat—thankfully not the floor—but his wipeout benefits me. He grabs at the air and almost catches my skirt, which he would have used to hold me back. I screech like a teenager being chased by a horny boy.

His feet slam the floor behind me as we race to the master bathroom. I make it through the door first and leap into the tub and sprawl out on the bottom. We both gasp for breath and laugh hysterically.

He leans on the counter and pants. "You start the water and I'll go shut the front door. I'd hate to discover a raccoon wandering around and causing havoc in the kitchen."

"You have to admit that would be funny!" I climb out of the tub and sit on the ledge.

"It would, but…" He crosses the room, palms my chin, and kisses me. "But I plan on making love to you in our bed tonight and not chase a raccoon around the house."

Bash makes good on his promise to make love to me. We connected on a much deeper level than we ever have. At one point, I couldn't tell where I ended and he began. We were one. My heart was so full. I cried and I don't know why.

As I lie beside him and watch his eyes shift beneath his lids, as if he were watching a movie as he sleeps, I can't help but feel my heart break for him.

Why does he choose to love only me and yet I share my heart with two others? Why doesn't it hurt him when he sees me in the throes of passion at their doing? Why do I allow it? How can I be so cruel to him?

He's so good to me and loves me without limitation. I love him. I do.

And I love Patch. Mack also holds a special place in my heart. Each man loves me differently; no one is better than the other, just different. I desire all of them.

All I know is that I don't deserve him.

CHAPTER FIVE

It's a warm, sunny day and I'm swimming with the Bear brothers in the river. The sunlight reflects off the water like it would an immaculate diamond. I can feel their love and respect for one another.

The men look into my eyes. Each reaches into my soul, taking pieces to keep for himself. They don't realize they're breaking me. They take and take, but it's Patch who grabs the biggest piece. He smiles boastfully at his prize until it begins to crack.

Every piece of me shatters into a million tiny shards and slowly floats downstream. I pull the broken pieces of myself back together and reach for a rock. I look back and expect to see all three men, but only Mack remains.

Broken pieces of Patch and Bash float past me. I reach for them but I'm unsure which pieces I should collect. I grab at them as they float away. I open my hand and expect to see many shards, but it's empty.

I startle when my alarm rudely interrupts the bizarre dream before I can figure out the message it brings, if any. I sit up quickly and search for Bash but he's not here. He likely already left for work at the paper.

My pajama top is stuck to my sweat-soaked skin, so I pull it over my head and toss it in the hamper as I make my way to the coffee pot. I'm thankful Bash left me half a pot still hot on the burner. He must have forgotten to fill his travel mug to sip during his drive into town.

After I peek through the window to ensure nobody's outside, I take my shirtless self and my coffee onto the porch to watch the sun reflect off the lazy river a mere hundred feet from where I sit. My dream weighs heavy in my thoughts, but I tilt my face toward the sun and feel my sorrows melt away.

***

My six-hour shift at the hospital zips by. I've been in surgery most of the time, which excites me. Lizzy and I have assisted Dr. Kacey for a few weeks. He doesn't have much of a sense of humor and glares at us when we joke around. He's hard to get to know and strikes me as a lonely old man.

Lizzy is hilarious; always cracks jokes, does ridiculous things, and chooses to wear the goofiest cartoon nurse's shirts. She's wacky and I love her.

We enter the female staff locker room together. Lizzy's locker is three down from mine. She flips hers open and snatches her phone from her purse. Her fingers tap and her eyes stare at the screen, she sits but only one buttock lands on the bench. In my peripheral, I see her topple over. She lands on the hard floor on her hip and shoulder.

"Oh, my God! Are you all right?" I reach out to grab her but she doesn't accept my hand because she's still typing on her phone. Her face is red from laughter. "Why are you laughing?"

She finally looks away from her phone and bursts into uncontrollable laughter. I laugh because it's contagious. Soon, both of us drip tears on our flushed faces. I sit on the bench and cross my legs to stop myself from peeing. When I voice my struggle, Lizzy snorts and curls into a ball, hoping to alleviate the painful tummy muscle spasms.

Eventually, we settle down and Lizzy plops her entire ass on the bench. She asks, "What are you up to later?"

I swap my nursing shoes for my street shoes. "I don't have any set plans." I glance at the clock on the wall. "Mack's gone back to the worksite. Bash is working at the paper and I don't know when he'll be home. I'm going to get one of the spare rooms ready because Patch might spend the night. We asked him to move in."

"Oh, yeah? Lucky girl!" She tilts her head and bats her eyelashes. "I know what you're going to be doing later." She rocks her hips on the bench and moans. "Oh, yes! Fuck me! Harder, baby!" She clutches her breasts and throws her head back. "Make me cum! Make me c—"

She halts when Kate, a much older nurse, appears from behind the row of lockers wearing an angry expression. "That is inappropriate for the workplace! Behave yourselves, ladies."

She disappears around the corner and we bite our lips to prevent from erupting into another fit of laughter.

"That woman needs to get laid," I whisper.

Lizzy repeats her sexy bucking, silently this time. She stops when I slap her arm playfully. She feigns severe pain and rubs her arm while she playfully sulks.

"You should meet the guys, especially Patch," I suggest with a wink.

She stops humping the bench to flash me a *whatever* expression.

I smile and tilt my head. "He'd really like you."

She squints. "Why? I mean, not why would he like me, because, shit…" She pauses to showcase her body by waving her hands up and down her torso. "Look at this body! I'm a hot little number." She bursts into laughter. "Seriously? Why would he like me when he has you? I mean, fuck, look at you!" Her hands gesture toward my body.

"Thank you," I say as I finger-brush back a lock of hair that slipped free from my ponytail a few hours ago and has been irritating me ever since. "Patch has a thing for redheads. At least, that's what Mack told me. His ex is a redhead. I've never met her."

She stands and fusses with her bags in her locker, then shoves her phone in her purse. "And if he likes me, and I like him, then what?" She stands with her hands perched on her hips.

I shrug. "He could do a lot worse." She stands tall and smiles proudly, then tips her head to thank me. "If the feelings were mutual," I pause to make sure I mean what I'm about to say, "go for it."

Her eyes assess my face for a hint of humor but she doesn't find it. "You would be okay if I fucked him?"

I nod. "Yeah, I think so. I mean, they're allowed to have relationships with other women as long as they're upfront about it and don't hide it. Protection is a must."

She tilts her head and assesses me. "Are you hoping I'll date him or should I just fuck him? And don't you think that would put a strain on our friendship?"

I consider her question while I tuck that hair back again, but it only falls free the moment I release it. "I really like you. You're honest and upfront about everything. You're well-grounded and mature yet still a toddler." She curls her lips inward and smiles to show all of her front teeth—something a child would do. "See, you're a toddler but you're a fun toddler. You're my best friend."

"Okay, so if I hopped on his lap and started making out with that huge hunk of a man—at least, I think he's massive if I judge by your pictures—you'd be fine with it?"

"He is massive, and yeah, I think so."

She shakes her head. "Well, I'm not ready to be in a steady relationship with anyone at the moment."

"I can respect that. What are your plans for the rest of the afternoon?" I ask while I twist the loose lock and tuck it beneath the hair that's conformed to my wishes. It'll look weird but I don't care at this point.

She shrugs. "Nothing much. My mom's been on a tirade lately, so I'd rather not go home. She didn't get the promotion she was seeking. I might go shopping to burn up some time. Besides, I could use some new bras." She pulls off her shirt and jostles her bra straps. "This one's old and stretched out.

My boobies are supporting the bra, not the other way around. You should come with! We can make an evening out of it."

I place my shoes in my locker, take out my purse and fling the strap over my shoulder. I'm trying not to look at her nearly nude breasts. I glance at her face but my sights drop to her bra. My tummy flutters and I jolt my eyes away. I look in my locker and collect my sweater, and then close and lock it.

"Are you embarrassed by my tits?" She scoffs and lowers her voice after realizing she said that rather loud. "You have sex with three men regularly and you're embarrassed by my bra-laden female breasts? What's wrong with you?" She scoffs again and drops her shirt.

"You're a girl." I turn toward her and bow. "You have very nice breasts." I finally meet her eyes. "Drop it, okay?"

"Fine!" she mutters and rolls her eyes. "Thanks for the compliment. I love my little titties." She gropes her breasts, and that's my cue to depart.

"See you!" I say as I fling open the door and walk through. I get halfway down the corridor and turn around. When I get back into the locker room, she's dressed in a form-fitted white camisole and a dark red zip-up hoodie. She's wiggling into a pair of faded, torn at the knee, snug-fitting jeans.

"You're back!" she says with surprise and slips her arms through the straps of her backpack and jostles it into place. "Did you change your mind and want to see my tits again?" She shakes her shoulders and they jiggle.

"No!" My eyes scan her breasts hidden beneath the white shirt. It's obvious she isn't wearing a bra because her nipples stand at attention. "Why don't you come to my house? We keep saying we're going to get together outside of work but we never do. We're both free tonight. Why not now? I mean, if your titties can bear holding up the bra for one more day."

She debates, but only for a few seconds. "Yeah, okay, but I'm not wearing the bra!" She opens the door and I walk through with her in tow. "I'll follow you. I'm parked in the back."

"Me too," I reply.

She slips her arm in mine and yammers on about how excited she is to finally see my house that I've told her all about but she's only seen in photos.

CHAPTER SIX

Nobody's home when we pull in. Lizzy parks her burgundy Jeep beside my car and gets out while she looks in awe at the house. I gather my bag and lead the way up the porch. I love her reaction. I'm so proud of this house.

"Oh, my God! You lucky bitch! Look at this fucking place! It's like...." She turns and spots the river through the clearing. "It's fucking beautiful here. How can you stand it?"

"Come on in," I shout to get her attention before she wanders toward the river.

She ascends the stairs while admiring the exterior and the hand-carved front door. "Oh, that's it! I'm moving in!"

"You might have to share a bed with Patch since he's moving in, too."

"That might be fun!" She laughs. "He's fucking hot in your pictures. He has this naughty bad boy look about him."

I set my bag on the bench near the door and she follows suit. She slips out of her shoes but leaves them where someone might trip on them. Patch will surely scowl and place them properly if he comes home.

Lizzy follows me as I show her around the house and gush at how much I love the guys for their kindness. She's in awe of the woodwork. She claims that Patch could make a killing by selling to people. I explain that he's too humble to take more money than he thinks is fair.

After I show her the upstairs and the living room, we head to the kitchen where I pour us each a glass of white wine. I show her the rooms and conclude the tour in the master bedroom. She stands just inside the door and bites her lip while she stares at the dark red, duvet-covered, king-size bed.

She sips her wine and whispers, "So, this is where all the magic happens."

Her sideways grin and dreamy eyes have me wishing I could read her thoughts. What is she picturing? Does she imagine herself being mauled by one Bear brother or all three? Or does she see me naked and lost in the pleasures of three sinfully sexy men?

I clear my throat to get her attention. Her cheeks flush. She sips her wine and follows me into the bathroom. As soon as she enters, her face lights up. She sets her wine on the counter between the double sinks and climbs into the huge tub. She lies back as if she were soaking her weary bones.

"Would you like to take a bath? You're welcome to," I say with a smile. "Bath sheets are in the closet. Salts and multiple essential oils are over there; personally, I favor the Lavender."

She sits up and stares through the large one-way window beside the tub. "I might never leave this tub if I lived here."

"It's a good thing you don't live here then." I shrug when she looks at me questioningly. "You'd be a shriveled mess." We both laugh as she climbs out.

We sink ourselves into the Adirondack chairs on the deck and sip our refilled wine glasses. The alcohol eases away the anxieties of the workday.

The sun hovers low in the sky when Patch's truck pulls in. He parks behind my car but ogles us as he exits his truck.

As he lazily struts toward the porch with a duffle bag slung over his shoulder, he looks sexier than I've ever seen him. It's not that he looks any different than he does any other day, but the way Lizzy's breath catches has me admiring him as the sexy being I know him to be.

His faded, snug-fit jeans do nothing to hide the bulge of his groin, nor his thick, muscular thighs or firm round ass. His shirt is draped over his shoulder beneath the bag's strap. In the rare places his skin isn't smudged with dirt, he glistens with the sweat from a hard day's work. He has a five o'clock shadow that I'm sure he'll take care of soon since he prefers to be smoothly shaven.

She whispers under her breath. "Oh. My. God!" She looks wide-eyed at me before her gaze returns to him. "*That's* Patch?"

"Yes, ma'am," I reply as his worn-in steel-toed boots thump with each step up the stairs.

He tosses the bag toward the door and it lands with a thud. His eyes are fixed on Lizzy. I don't blame him; she's gorgeous and her fiery red hair glimmers in the sagging evening sun.

Despite her efforts to appear nonchalant, she clutches the armrests of her Adirondack chair and swallows hard. Her eyes follow his every step.

Patch's attention directs to me. He leans in and kisses my lips tenderly.

I ask, "Who's bike do you have in the back of your truck?"

He looks at the black and silver crotch-rocket. As if remembering something upsetting, his brow scrunches and he sighs heavily. "It's Mack's."

"I didn't know he had a bike?"

"It's been in the shed in desperate need of repairs for a few years. I didn't think he'd ever want to ride again after someone clipped him and it nearly wrote the bike off. He kept all of his skin thanks to his leathers but he broke some fingers. He was bruised all down his left side." He groans as he looks at the bike. "Anyway, since he's out of town he called to ask if I could pick it up at the shop."

I shake my head. "I don't like it."

"Me either, but he's a grown man." He sits in the chair across from Lizzy, leans back, and scans her up and down. "And who might you be?" His voice is deep with an easiness to it that has her thighs squeezed together. He crosses his feet but his knees are spread. One hand rests on his thick thigh and the other rests on the armrest.

I clear my throat. "Patch, meet my friend Lizzy. We work together at the hospital. You've heard me talk about her on more than one occasion."

"I can finally put a beautiful face to the name." He leans forward to stretch his hand toward her while his eyes blaze into hers. "Hello, Lizzy." Her name rolls off his tongue.

"Hi." She shakes his hand. He hesitates before he releases it. She clears her throat, slips her hand from his, and snuggles back into the chair. "You built an incredible home. It's fabulous."

His hand—stained with dirt from a hard day's work—strokes his thigh, drawing her eyes down toward his bulging crotch. He's testing her with subtle gestures to see if she'll show a sexual interest in him. Either that or he's simply toying with her. She's fallen right into his trap, and the twitch of his lips proves it.

He asks, "What's your favorite thing about this house, Lizzy?"

She looks up from his thigh and fixes her eyes on me. "The tub, I think." She smiles wide and her cheeks flush.

"She hopped in it. I said she could take a bath but—"

"If I did, I'd still be in it." Her smile shows off her beautiful white teeth which have Patch licking his lips.

"So, Lizzy…" He sits forward, and she looks wide-eyed at him. He takes my glass of wine and sips it while he seduces her with his dominant demeanor. "What brings you home with our Goldie?"

"I had nothing to do and considered going bra shopping but…" She pauses when she notices his eyes locked on her breasts. Her nipples are like heat-seeking missiles aimed for Patch. "As you can see, I didn't go."

His eyes jerk back to meet hers. He tips his head as if to say touché. She got one up on him and he's intrigued. There's definitely a connection between them. Any concerns I might have about jealousy are quashed by my naughty thoughts.

"Don't ever cover those gorgeous breasts. And you're welcome to visit any time. You can take a bath or sunbathe nude with Goldie, should that tickle you just right." One side of his lip twists just slightly. Fucking hell, he's sexy!

"Will it only be Goldie and I who'll be nude or will you be in your birthday suit, too?" she asks with playful innocence in her tone.

"Just say the word, little girl." He tips his head to look at her from under the shadow of his brows. His lascivious grin screams naughty thoughts and my breath catches.

She stutters, "I—I'll keep that in mind."

He snickers because he knows the effect he has on her. "I'm going to take a shower."

Patch stands and I see the bulge of his semi-hard cock from behind the denim. I tip my head back as he leans in. His face hovers above mine and his eyes are riddled with questions, especially after I wave an eyebrow. His lips press to mine more aggressively than when he first arrived.

He asks, "Have you had anything to eat or have set dinner plans?" I lift my wineglass, snicker, and then shake my head. He tilts his face toward Lizzy, who studies his every move. "You're staying for dinner."

She nods and he smiles, then collects his bag and saunters into the house.

Her mouth hangs open. She gulps the last of her second glass of wine and bursts into hushed laughter. "Holy fuck! You weren't kidding! That man is intense! No wonder you look exhausted all the time. How are you able to walk after that huge stallion humps you?" She lies back in the chair and fans herself with the hand that doesn't hold the spent wine glass.

I down mine and put my hand out to collect her glass. She hands it to me and debates on another since she plans to drive home later. She'll be here for a while longer so she accepts another refill.

While I'm in the house, Bash pulls in and parks his old truck beside Lizzy's Jeep. He hops out and strides to the porch with his long legs. He doesn't see her on the porch.

"Hi," she says. I hear her through the open window.

He stops just before he reaches the door. "Oh, hi! Sorry, I didn't see you sitting there." He approaches her with his hand out. "I'm Bash Bear. You are?"

She stands just enough to be gracious and shakes his hand before she sits back. "I'm Lizzy. I work with Goldilocks at the hospital."

I watch them through the window while I open a second bottle of wine.

He smiles. "I've heard some stories. She talks about you a lot. Only good things, I assure you." He sits on the chair Patch just vacated. "Goldie in the house?" Lizzy nods. "It's nice to put a face to the name. You're a sight to behold. Sorry if that was out of line."

She spreads her arms wide. "What woman doesn't like compliments?"

His voice lowers to where I have to listen harder to hear what he says. "I want to thank you for your kindness toward Goldie. Few people are nice to her when they learn of her relationship with us *evil* Bear brothers. We're assholes, in case you haven't heard."

"I don't listen to the masses. I'd rather go by what Goldilocks tells me." She fiddles with a lock of her hair.

"What does she tell you?" He tilts his head and crinkles his forehead in the same manner as Patch when he tries to search someone's eyes for answers.

I can't see her face. "To be honest, she's told me about her relationship with all three of you—not right away, of course. It took her a while to open up. She didn't give in-depth details but I know she's intimate with all of you and you have an open relationship."

"Semi-open," he corrects.

The sound of the wine filling her glass prevents me from hearing what she says. After I fill both glasses, I get a beer from the fridge for Bash.

"Yes, if permission is granted," I hear him say as I walk through the door.

"Thank you." He takes the beer I offer and then kisses me when I lean in.

"Permission granted?" I ask as I hand her a full wine glass.

She replies, "Bash was just explaining the rules to your relationship when it comes to other partners."

He says, "I explained that we can't just hop into bed with anyone. Its permission granted only."

"It is now," I say to him, then go on to explain to Lizzy. "Mack started dating Shaina while I was away at school. Bash had sex with her and hesitated to tell me. I found out from Mack and it went to shit. So, now it's a permission-granted thing between Bash and me. If Patch and Mack want to have sex with someone else, they can, but they have to tell us about it out of respect for us."

Lizzy gulps some wine. "I'm secretly jealous that Goldilocks has three amazing men who love her and I don't even have one." She tips her glass toward me. "You deserve them. This girl is fucking amaze-balls. Beautiful and smart!"

She points her finger at me. "I love this woman. She's deserving of only the best life can offer. I wish the whole world could see that." Lizzy is chatty from the alcohol.

"She certainly does," he says.

Lizzy leans toward me. "You're my best friend. Did you know that?"

I blow a kiss at her and notice Bash's sights are on her chest while he licks his lips.

She continues. "I mean it. I've never had a friend that doesn't judge me or get upset with me if her boyfriend checks me out. I'm small and bubbly, so sue me! I can't stop someone from looking at me. I would never get upset if my boyfriend—" She pauses and looks at Bash. "Not that I have a boyfriend.

I don't. They were all assholes and I kicked them to the curb. Well, I still live with my mom and didn't actually live with the guys, but you know what I mean."

He interrupts her. "From what I can tell, you're lovely. Every woman should be adored by her man. He should put her above himself, always, and treat her with the same respect she shows him. Fuck those assholes. They don't deserve you."

"Goldilocks, if he wasn't your boyfriend I'd hop on his lap and make out with him. I totally would." She growls when Bash smiles and shows off his perfect white teeth. She waves her finger at Bash. "He's the sweetest and sexiest fucker I've seen in a long time. I mean, other than the stud in the house who's an older and more dangerous version of this one."

If he doesn't want me to catch him checking her out, he's lousy at concealing it. To fuck with him, I look at her and say, "You can hop on his lap if he says it's okay."

In my peripheral, I see his head jerk in my direction, but I'm too entertained by Lizzy's questioning eyes to look at him. She glances at him, then back at me, and bursts into laughter. I meet his squinted eyes and laugh too, then I sip my wine.

Patch steps outside wearing the low-rise faded blue jeans that look great on him. He didn't bother with a shirt or shoes. He swigs from his beer as he strolls toward us. As per typical Patch fashion, he smells great!

"I'm thinking of throwing some deer steaks on the grill. Lizzy, you like deer? I killed it myself."

"Gun?" she questions.

"Bow and arrow is my personal preference, not that I think a gun is evil or anything. I simply like the challenge of a bow."

Lizzy can hardly take her eyes off Patch's abs while he struts from the barbecue to the kitchen and back. With her distracted, Bash gets my attention. His eyebrows furrow and I wink at him, which intensifies his questioning leer.

CHAPTER SEVEN

After dinner, Patch wanted to drop Mack's bike back at the main house. Lizzy wanted to tag along and Patch was more than happy for the company. They won't be gone long unless he takes her in the house to show her around where he'll likely put his moves on her—not that he'd have to work too hard at it. She looks at him like a thirsty man looks at an ice-cold beer.

Bash and I tidy the kitchen. He's quiet for a few minutes as he waves his fingers under the stream of water, waiting for it to warm up. His eyes haven't veered from me as I clear the table.

I put my hands on my hips. "Stop staring! You're creeping me out."

He smiles. "I'm glad I can still make you quiver." I scrunch my face as if undecided if that's true. "So, what was that about earlier?"

"What was what about?" I ask as I circle the table to collect the silverware.

He sets the plates into the growing suds. "You know what I'm talking about. Lizzy. Outside. You … saying it was okay if she sat on my lap and made out with me."

He straightens when I stand next to him and look up at his eyes. "Oh, that!" I jest with a smirk and a wave of my eyebrows.

"Yes, that." He licks his lips. "What were you hoping would happen?"

I shrug and turn to walk away but he grabs my arm with his sudsy hand. I yip and he pulls me close to him and holds the back of my neck to keep me in place.

He looks down at me with heavily lidded eyes and speaks slowly. "What would you have done if she had taken you up on your offer?"

"Ummmmm…" I pause to consider the possibilities and to make him wait. "I would have sat and watched."

He leans back enough that he can assess my face to see if I'm serious. "Do you think you'd like to watch me fuck your friend?"

My pussy twitches. "I might be okay with that. I mean, I really like Lizzy. She's sexy as hell, witty, intelligent and I know she doesn't have unprotected sex with anyone. When I picture you with another girl, I don't see you with Shaina even though you two did it. That's weird, right?" I don't give him a chance to answer. "I'm not going to lie; I get a little aroused when I imagine Lizzy moan as you bend her over a table and slide your massive cock into her tiny body."

He's looking over my head and wears a quirky grin as if picturing himself in that exact scenario. His smile fades. "But when it would be all said and done, you still have to work with her, she'll still be your friend and you'll never get that image of us out of your mind. What if it doesn't work out well? Are you willing to lose her as a friend?"

I'm quiet while I wet the washcloth and make my way to the table, while I consider what he's proposing. He shuts off the water and picks up the first plate and washes it, then runs it under the clean water before he sets it on the rack. I can feel his eyes on me as he waits for me to answer.

"I think our friendship is stronger than that. We both have a mature way of looking at relationships, and she's the type of person who resolves issues and doesn't let them fester. She's not shy about speaking her mind, but she'll listen to opposition and consider whether or not she's right."

With his hands sunk in the bubbles, he pauses to look at me as I lean on the fridge a few feet from him. "If I had sex with her, would you watch, or do you want to be involved…" he pauses. "Or would you like to have sex with her, too?"

He sets a plate on the rack. I point and say, "You didn't rinse that."

"What?" he asks, then discovers a wad of bubbles gliding down the plate. He rinses it and dries his hand on the towel he slung over his shoulder earlier. With one hand on the sink's edge and the other on his hip, he patiently waits for me to answer.

I flip my hands out from my sides and, with a voice higher than usual, reply. "I don't know! I—I don't know. I mean, maybe I would." My face flushes hot. "I might try it one day but what if I get down there," I gesture toward an imaginary Lizzy's vagina "and I gag? She'd be so insulted!"

"If you don't like it, you can gesture to me and I'll take over. I love eating pussy." Bash steps toward me and lifts my chin so he can look into my eyes. "You aren't ready to take that step. One step at a time, okay? There's no rush. If you decide to—and I really want you to think about it when you're sober—we can invite her to our bed. But that isn't going to happen tonight, so let's just enjoy ourselves. Shall we?"

I shake my head. "Definitely not tonight. I believe she and Patch are going at it right now."

He looks surprised. "Do you think?"

I nod emphatically. "Did you see how she was looking at him? Oh, man! That girl's hot for him." I close the distance between us. "Besides, I told her she could fuck him if she wants to."

"You did? Hmm…" He mumbles, "I'll have to ask him if she's as much of a firecracker as I imagine she would be."

"Well, fill me in after you find out." I smirk and slap his ass as I pass him to go to the washroom.

He adds, "I'm sure Patch will take the lead, and the poor girl won't stand a chance."

"He's definitely dominant."

Patch's truck pulls in and parks in the same place as earlier, less the motorcycle in the back. He hops out and jogs around the front of the truck in hopes of being a gentleman by opening her door. But before he can assist, she has both feet on the ground and the door slams shut. She's a little bouncier with each step and I catch his fleeting smile.

He likes her!

She comes through the door waving a bottle of red wine over her head. "Since we finished the last one, we brought another. Crack it open, woman!" She hands it to me with her eyes wide. She mouths the words, "Oh, my God!"

I whisper, "I thought you'd be gone longer than that." She shrugs and feigns innocence. "I figured you'd be all over him."

She sports a crooked smile. "As much as I'd like to, it would be weird. He's your man; it just seems wrong."

I roll my eyes. "It's a permission-granted situation, as you know, and I gave you permission in the locker room. Don't you remember?"

She scoffs. "That was just locker room talk. I didn't think you were serious."

"Okay," I say as I draw out the word. "Well," I pause to pick up the corkscrew. "Consider this an official permission granting conversation." I wink and she takes a step back.

She stands tall and turns at her waist to look at the boys who've perched themselves at the dining room table with their beers. Their voices are low, and I see Patch point to the picture he hung for me.

She spins back and says, "In that case, sadly, I may have missed my opportunity. He probably thinks I'm not interested because I didn't try to kiss him in the truck. I had the chance after he took the bike out of the back." Her eyes widen. "Fuck, he's strong!"

"Girl, you have no idea. If you two hook-up, he'll toss you around like you're a ragdoll." We both laugh when Lizzy waves her arms and does a little jig as if she were a floppy doll. I hand her a filled glass. "Listen, he's not shy. If he's interested, he'll let you know."

Bash breaks out a deck of cards. He assigns Patch and Lizzy to be teammates. He says it's because he wants to be across the table from me so he can look at his one true love. Lizzy fakes a wretch and Patch snickers. I pay them no attention because I adore Bash's mushy sentiment.

After too many Euchre games to count where Patch and Lizzy kicked our asses, we're all a little intoxicated. The old clock with the crooked hands *pings* to alert us to how late it is. The sound is like a spoon tapping an empty tin can. One day I'll get a clock that chimes like a clock should.

Patch grunts. "Well, I have to turn in. Morning comes early around here." He gulps the remainder of beer from his bottle.

Bash turns his body to look at the clock, even though he could just count the number of pathetic pings. "Yeah, me too."

"Lizzy," I say while I lean my elbows on the table. Bash listens intently. "You have to spend the night. There's no way in hell I'm going to let you drive."

With a sexier voice than his already sexy voice, Patch says, "You can sleep in my bed." She tilts her head to look his way. "Don't worry, I'll climb in with Goldilocks and Bash. We can sandwich the poor girl."

"It's like sleeping between two actual bears and not just two guys bearing the name Bear," I say with a laugh that's a little over the top—thanks to the multiple glasses of wine and two beers. "Pardon the pun!"

She laughs so hard she snorts. Somehow, she manages to say, "That was so *punny*!"

It takes a few minutes before we calm down. I think the guys were laughing at our silliness but they laughed, and that's what counts.

Lizzy stands and sucks back the last swallow of wine, then hands her glass to Bash. "I'm always cold, boys!" She waves her fingers as if to suggest they warm her up. She's giddy so she can't stop giggling, which ruins the sexy suggestion—whether she meant it or not.

Patch puts his hand out to take hers. She glints and grabs it. "Come with me," he says without even a hint of a smile. "Let me take you to my bed."

I tease with a long "O" sound! She follows him while she laughs and humps her hips toward him. She looks hilarious. He doesn't see because she's behind him.

Bash runs his fingers through his thick, dark brown hair and erupts into laughter. Patch looks at him to see what's so funny. She stops humping before he sees her, and she turns her head like she's trying to find out why Bash laughed. It draws his attention from her. He discovers nothing comical and pulls her along.

Bash mumbles. "Patch isn't going to make it to our bed tonight, is he?"

I look at him with my hands clasped behind my back and a wide smile I can't seem to ease. "No, he won't."

He takes my hand and leads me through the living room and then the kitchen to shut off lights as we make our way to the bedroom. He helps me out of my dress before we reach the bed. I giggle when he undoes my bra with two fingers quicker than I ever could. I walk backward as my panties shimmy down my legs. I step out of them while he slowly saunters toward me with glassy eyes and an alcohol-induced smile. The darkened room casts shadows over his face that would have me question my decision to be alone with him if I didn't know him well.

He leans in to kiss me but before he can, I whisper, "I have to pee."

"Of course, you do." He looks toward the heavens and points to the bathroom.

When I return, he's lying on the bed with the covers pulled back. He pats the empty spot beside him. I slip in and he flips the covers over me just as my lips find his. I roll onto him and straddle his thighs. I kiss and lick from his lips down to his erection.

I take the spongy mushroom head in my hand so I can tease the slit with the tip of my tongue and taste his arousal. He moans with appreciation. His hands slip under the sheet and gather my hair gently to hold it out of my way. My head bobs under the sheet as my lips glide up and down his shaft.

"Goldie, babe," he pants. "Come up here."

My puffy lips peck at his nipples. His hands cradle my face and urge me up so he can kiss me. Our tongues dance slowly as I position myself over his shaft and slowly sink down onto him. I take every inch.

I moan into his mouth as I begin bucking forward and back, rubbing my clitoris along his tight tummy. Back and forth. Back and forth. I set the pace to ease myself toward climax. There's no need to rush. I want our bond to last.

With one of his hands on the back of my neck and the other spanned across my ass cheek, I buck above him, and rock increasingly faster as the tightness in my tummy builds as if a balloon inflates in the most deliriously mind-numbing way. I grind my body as hard as I can to take every inch of him. My slick juices allow my clit to glide easily along his flesh.

The room spins and everything tightens inside my tummy from my clit to my belly button. The room spins. My feet slide under his thighs and hold tightly. Otherwise, I'll surely float away. My lungs burn and my tits ache from bouncing…

But the balloon swells inside me and it's almost more than I can bear. Suddenly, the earth stills. My mind falls dark. My body is no longer mine. I'm afloat.

My entire body jerks as if my soul has slammed its way back in. His hand over my mouth muffles my scream. At the moment, I don't care if I never breathe again.

His hand falls away and my gasp is met with his deepthroated, lengthy groan. His body stills beneath me as his hands squeeze my ass cheeks and pin me against him. His cock swells and stretches my walls as my pussy twitches with appreciation.

Slowly, his muscles ease and I collapse against him and bury the bridge of my nose against his neck. We lie unmoved until our breathing eases. My legs ache so I lift my weary body to release his withering penis along with his spent cum.

Just as I get to my feet, movement in the shadows catches my eye and I screech. "Patch! Holy fuck! You scared me. Why are you hiding?"

He laughs as he stands from the chest he sat on. "Well, I didn't want to interrupt such a beautiful moment." I can't tell if he's being sarcastic or if he enjoyed his voyeuristic moment.

"Well, it's over now so you can climb in," Bash groans and rolls onto his side and punches the pillow to fluff it.

I say, "I'm going to take a shower."

Bash says, "I can't believe you sat there and watched. Pervert!" He throws the pillow at Patch but he bats it off course and launches it back with perfect precision.

I shut the door and shower. When I step out, Bash slips in. I dry off and slide into bed with my butt snuggled against Patch's tummy. He brushes my hair off my cheek, then kisses my neck. "I love you, Goldie."

"I know you do," I whisper. "I love you, too."

He takes a deep breath. "I like Lizzy. She's fun and she doesn't take my shit, much like someone else I know."

"Who, me?" I ask as innocently as I can manage without laughing. "No, I'm a total pushover."

"You know you push my buttons. You fucking live for that shit." He kisses just behind my ear. "Lizzy has that same defiant glint in her eye as you which is probably why you two get along so well. Your glint is more dangerous."

"Dangerous?" I question and turn my face toward the ceiling and try to look over my shoulder.

"Dangerous because it makes me fall. As great as that is, I know you could just as easily break me."

I reach down and lift his heavy arm from my waist and pull it up between my breasts. "If you want Lizzy, I already gave her the okay."

"You did?" he asks with surprise in his tone.

"She didn't tell you?" I ask but he shakes his head. "Bash and I talked about it—and it's just talk at this point—but we're considering letting her join the group. I mean, if it's okay with you and Mack, of course. I'm not sure if I'm ready to be with her—like, me, myself—but the thought of one of you fucking her while I watch is intriguing."

He yawns just as Bash opens the bathroom door and shuts out the light, returning the room to its darkened state. He slides in beside me. I reach toward him and find his hand and weave my fingers in his.

"Goodnight. I love you guys," I whisper. Both men return the sentiment and I'm quick to sink into a deep sleep.

CHAPTER EIGHT

Something wakes me. A heavy arm resting over my waist has me pinned beneath the sheets. Going by the tattoo, it's Bash's arm. Patch isn't in bed in front of me where he was when I fell asleep. I use the utmost care not to wake Bash. He doesn't even stir.

I hear something. With the silence of a mouse, I make my way toward the noise. Before I arrive at the scene, something stills me. Although muffled, the sounds are obvious in nature; moans. My pussy twitches and my heart pounds faster.

I peek around the corner and hope they won't see me.

She's on her back on the island with her legs bent at the knee, spread wide and her calves dangle over the edge. Patch's huge hands have pinned her wrists to the counter beside her hips and his face is buried between her thighs.

My nipples are desperate to poke through the oversized t-shirt I tossed on before I left the bedroom. She's wearing Patch's red t-shirt. It's pulled up to her neck, exposing her breasts. They're small, perky, and perfect; much nicer than mine.

Her head flops to her right and I duck back behind the wall. If she'd seen me, she'd surely have reacted in some way, and since her moans continue to seduce my ears, I doubt she saw me.

I hear the squeal of skin scrape along the counter. I know exactly what's happening; he doesn't want her to cum until he's inside her. He'll fuck her and make her wait for her release. I peek again.

She whispers, "What the fuck, Patch?" Her breath rushes from her as if she's being manhandled. "I was almost there."

"Shush." Patch's whisper, as low and deep as it is, makes my tummy flutter and surely hers as well.

I peek again just as she asks, "What?" but doesn't protest when he lifts her up and spins her mid-air, then sets her on her feet. She grips the island while he rips a condom package with his teeth and tosses the package to the floor which is not in typical Patch OCD fashion. His jeans are in a heap on the floor beside him while he rolls the condom onto his erection.

His hand covers her mouth while he holds her back against his chest. He whispers in her ear but I can hear. "You'll cum when I allow it. Grab the edge and hold on. I'm going to fuck you how you deserve to be fucked."

She leans forward but doesn't pull his hand from her mouth. She must like to be muffled.

He pushes his cock deep into her in one thrust. If it weren't for his hand, she surely would have screamed. He pulls out and she abruptly pushes back on him. She wants more. Even though I can't see his face, Patch surely sports a wicked grin.

He pulls her head back while he presses on her lower back which forces her into an arch. She's quite flexible.

In her ear, he whispers. "You want to fuck hard, little girl?" She nods enthusiastically. "If you want me to stop, wave your hand because I'm not letting go of your mouth. I'd bet you're a screamer and I'm not about to share you tonight. You're mine! You're fucking mine!"

Patch grips her hip and continues to hold her mouth. His powerful thrusts have her at his mercy. He's rough, very rough just like when he is with me and wants to own my body. My clit twitches as I watch the mountainous man fuck Lizzy with a vengeance. Her feet aren't on the floor. He holds her by her hip and humps so hard that gravity seems to be at a loss.

She screams beneath his hand but doesn't wave to make it stop. Her muscles are flexed and her fingers are white from their death grip on the counter. She cries out when Patch's hand slips. The sound echoes about the kitchen. He covers her mouth and nose and pulls back until the back of her head rests against his chest. His hips retreat and his cock slips free.

He growls beside her ear. "No screaming!" Their heavy breaths are loud. "You scream, I stop. Do you understand?" She doesn't react. "Tell me you understand."

His hand remains in place but she tries to speak. She fails of course, but her laughter has him shaking his head; entertained by her humor. He releases her mouth.

Through her panted breaths, she says, "I understand just fine, Sir." Then curtseys.

"You're trouble! I fucking like trouble," he whispers, then grabs her hair and pulls her head back so he can kiss her mouth. She tries to turn her body but he won't allow it. He kicks her feet apart and she arches her back. He slips his cock back inside her pussy. His mouth muffles her moan. Damn, she's flexible!

To fuck her at a better angle, he pushes her head forward and bends her at her hips but continues his hold on her long red hair. His free hand slips down her tummy and finds her clitoris.

Oh, yes! My mind spins. I know exactly how she feels. He loves to get me off with his finger while he whispers naughty things and leisurely fucks me.

My fingers find my clit and begin to copycat his gentle massage, as I know is his way. I imagine him filling me, fucking me slowly so I can feel every inch of him glide along my walls. I bite my lips between my teeth to hold back my own pleasure. I want to hear her cum. She's perfectly still, as am I aside from my fingers—*his* fingers. Slowly, they rub and caress her—and me with my imagination—closer and closer to euphoria.

She covers her mouth with her palm to restrain her moan. She's coming. I want to cum too but I'm not there, yet. Her chest heaves and her legs shake as though she were supporting his weight as well as her own. She stills and her breath holds.

I step back and lean against the wall to continue my merciless assault on my own clitoris. My jaw clenches and the tingles build in my tummy until my clit numbs, but the numbness feels so perfect. I imagine how sensual she looks at the peak of her own climax. She cries out beneath her own hand and the air seems to still around me.

A thud yanks me back to reality. My knees are weak but I step forward to catch another glance. He's picked her up. Her arms and legs are wrapped around him and her back is against the refrigerator. He reaches around her ass to guide his cock into her pussy.

Patch wraps his thick forearm around her back to hold her against his chest. Their lips intertwine with a heated passion that would have Hollywood directors delirious. He carries her to the table and feels for a chair. He spins it, then turns and sits. He releases her back but quickly grips her ass with both hands to encourage her to ride him like a cowboy on a bucking bronco.

They're like wild animals. All I can do is stare at them and take notes. She's an aggressive lover, at least she is with Patch. I'm shocked the chair can withstand the severity of the assault. He reaches up and captures a lock of her red hair. She grips the back of his neck to keep her balance.

He tilts her head back and licks up her neck. She continues to ride his cock with more speed and power than I thought a woman her size could muster. Her movements become jerky, not nearly as consistent as they had been. She's coming!

"Cum on my cock. Good girl," Patch whispers against her neck. "Your cunt is fucking tight." He moans. "Oh yeah, squeeze my cock."

His erratic breaths halt, lips pull back to reveal clenched teeth. His face darkens and the veins on his forehead grow more prominent. She cries out just as he exhales with a throaty groan.

Their bodies seem to soften instantly. She cradles his face and kisses him tenderly. But only once.

"Thanks for the nightcap." She slides off his lap. "Good night, Patch."

She promenades to Patch's bedroom and leaves him seated on the chair and desperate to calm his breathing while his cock withers inside the spent condom. He snickers and sits with his hands on the back of his head. He knows he's been conquered.

I scurry quietly back to bed and slip in. I face a softly snoring Bash, who still hasn't shifted position. I want to wake him to tell him but it can wait.

Patch is nearly silent as he sneaks into the master bathroom and closes the door. A few moments pass before the sweet scent of body wash caresses my nostrils when his freshly cleansed body slides into bed behind me. His heavy arm slips beneath the sheet and flops over my waist. He pulls me back until I'm safely tucked against him.

"She's a firecracker," he whispers. "Isn't she?"

I turn my head and try to look at him but he has me too tightly against him. "How did you know I was watching?"

"I saw you."

"She's a wild woman, for sure." I can't help but smile. "I think she got the better of you."

His tummy tightens as if suppressing a laugh. "I think you're right."

I giggle louder than I should and Bash moans and rolls over. "Don't cry into a box of tissues if she doesn't call you in the morning."

"Good thing I'll be cooking her breakfast then, huh?"

CHAPTER NINE

Morning comes too quickly. I'm woken from a dream where Mack is licking my pussy and I was so close to orgasm. For a second, I'm angry that I'm awake but then it's wonderfully clear that someone is under the covers and doing exactly what Mack was in my dream.

Not to ruin the mystery, I don't lift the sheet to see who. Instead, I close my eyes and enjoy the sensations and think only of my clit and how hot and wet the tongue and lips are as they suck and lick every awakened nerve.

It isn't more than a minute before I clutch the sheet above the mystery person's head while I lift my hips to meet their laps. They suck, lap, and spin circles around my clit.

My entire body stills as the most pleasure any woman can feel overtake every cell of my being. All too soon, I fall back into my body and twitch with each torturous flick of the magical tongue on my hypersensitive clit.

The person's head glides under the sheet like a shark about to catch its prey. It glides free. Patch's lips are puffy and slick with my arousal. He kisses me and leaves my scent on my lips. I wipe my lips as he climbs off the bed. I expected he'd be naked but he's already wearing his jeans, no shirt, no socks.

He runs his palm over his rock-hard abs. "You should get up now. I'm making breakfast." He struts to the bathroom and washes his face while I sit up and slip the oversized t-shirt I wore last night back on.

"Is Lizzy up?" My throat is dry, making my tone deeper.

He pokes his head through the doorway. His face is lathered in soap. "No, not yet." He ducks back in.

I slip my feet into my fuzzy slippers and pass Patch. I watch him look at himself in the mirror as he dries his face. He looks like he just stepped off a military base; strong, stern, and in command. He exits the bathroom and I close the door. I pee, brush my teeth, and make my way to the kitchen.

After I've sipped from the mug Patch handed me with the cost of a kiss, I set it down on the table and shuffle my feet all the way to where Lizzy sleeps. I'm too tired to lift my unusually heavy legs.

After I tap lightly on the ajar door, I push it open. Lizzy is sprawled face down under the covers with her head buried under a pillow. I flop on the bed next to her and she jolts upright.

"What the fuck, bitch? Ouch!" Her hands press over her eyes and she groans. "Too. Bright. Head. Hurts."

Slightly louder than a whisper, I agree. "Yeah, we drank too much last night. It's not bright in here; it's a rainy day. Get up, you'll feel better after a hearty breakfast and some drugs." I roll toward her and she flips to face me. I grimace at how pale she is which emphasizes the purple bags beneath her eyes. "I thought Patch would have fucked the alcoholic stupor right out of you."

Her eyes widen in surprise but she quickly grimaces at the pain her reaction caused. "You already know about that? Is nothing sacred between you people?"

"Sorry to break it to you, but I watched most of it."

Her pale face flushes to make her look almost lifelike. She presses her face into the pillow. "Oh, my God! I'm so embarrassed!"

"Don't be! You were smoking hot. Damn, girl! I could never move like that." I yawn. "You put me to shame."

She turns her head and brushes the hair off her face. "Confession: I had to learn how to use my boyfriend's bodies how I wanted because try as they might, they couldn't satisfy me." She takes a breath and releases it slowly. "That man, Patch, can fuck!"

I nod and our laughs fill the room.

"On a more serious note; are you thinking about dating him?" I ask after I cough. My throat is still dry.

"No! He's your boyfriend. Well, one of them." She snickers. "When I got into bed last night, I felt like I'd betrayed you. I don't want to hurt you in any way."

"You didn't hurt me." I roll my eyes and sigh, embarrassed to tell her. "While I was watching him rub your clit, while he fucked you slowly, I masturbated."

Her smile widens. "You did?" She rolls onto her back and looks up at the ceiling. "That's so hot!"

"The scene was hot! He's had me exactly how you were— against the counter—so I know what you were experiencing, and it was exciting." My face feels hot.

Her brows lift in the center. "So, you're okay with what happened? Like, if it were to happen again…" Her words fall away but I can tell she hopes it will.

"You can play with him any time you'd like."

"Yay!" Her smile falls away. "I know all the guys like to share their toys, so what if Bash wants to play with me? I am a shiny new toy. That's not okay, is it?"

"I love the reference, and we are toys when it comes to their dicks. But no, it's not too far. I don't think it would bother me. He and I discussed the possibility of it happening sometime in the future. But if you're going to be with Bash, I would like to be there." I waggle my eyebrows. "Maybe I'll join in, and we can tag team him. I think he'd like that."

She taps her chin as if unsure, then nods emphatically. "He'd be a fool not to!" I sit up and she copies, with a groan. "If and when you're ready for that, you let me know. If you never want me to be with Bash, I'm fine with that, too. My worst fear is losing you as my best friend."

She stands and stretches as I make my way toward the door. "I'm not going anywhere. As long as you abide by the rules and don't lie about anything, I can't see there being a problem." I turn and point at her. "And don't get pregnant!"

"Ew!" She reacts as if I asked her to eat poop; she shivers clear into her soul. She follows me. "I don't want kids! No, thank you!"

"Never?" I ask and she emphatically shakes her head.

Before we enter the hallway, she lowers her voice. "*If* I ever were to have sex with Bash, and you don't want it to happen again, you'll tell me, right?"

"Of course!"

She yawns. "I have yet to meet Mack. In pictures, he's the cutest of the three. Sorry! That isn't to say Patch and Bash aren't hot as fuck because…" She raises her eyebrows and waves her arms as if to showcase them like they're right in front of her. "Fuck!"

"I know, Mack's *GQ* pretty," I say with a smile.

We enter the kitchen together and Patch takes notice. He whistles. "If you two aren't the most beautiful creatures I've ever seen…" He pauses to look us up and down. "Ladies, you're a sight to behold."

We both grimace and mumble about how awful we look and how hungover we are. I reach for the pill bottle while she takes the full mug from Patch. He doesn't lean in to kiss her but the way he looks at her commands submission. She glances at his strong abs and then winks at him but doesn't let him kiss her when he finally does lean in. She challenges his dominance and I try to hide my entertainment.

"Where's Bash?" she asks as she turns her back to Patch. She sips her coffee and sighs happily.

Patch lifts his shoulders in a half shrug then rubs his chin. "He left for work almost an hour ago."

CHAPTER TEN

It's been a few days since Lizzy spent the night. We're getting along superbly, and our dynamic at work is excellent. Neither of us feels awkward about her wild night with Patch. The only change is that we can talk on a more intimate level than before. I don't have to hold things back from her anymore.

When I asked her if she was going to call him and maybe go on a date, she told me that she doesn't want to get serious with anyone. She wants to fuck him again but keep it casual. I'm sure he'll be okay with that.

We discussed her having sex with Bash and decided to let the idea float around for a while. If the right moment hits, it'll be up to me to act upon it. If it never does that's okay too.

Lizzy and I have Friday off so I invite her to go to the mall with me to do some lingerie shopping and then to come over for some day drinking. She accepted with great enthusiasm.

My arm stretches along the cool sheet in search of Bash's hot body but the vacancy has me painfully aware of how much I miss him.

There's a note next to the half-full pot of coffee still perched on the burner. After I pour myself a steaming mug, I read the note.

Goldie, I had a meeting with Garrett at the Daily News, *then I'm going to meet up with Patch for some brother time. He wants to walk the forest to find the perfect tree for his projects. We might not be home until late. Mack is expected back from the site and promised to check in on you later. Have fun!*

P. S. I'm your most cherishing admirer!

I take my book and head outside to read on the porch. The sun is low on the horizon, promising to be a hot day. The sky is powder blue with cotton ball clouds. It's hard to believe they're calling for a heavy storm.

After two mugs of coffee, the sky darkens, and the wind whips. Time to head inside and do some housework. I shower, sweep the floor, do some dusting and start some laundry. It's only eleven o'clock and I'm already bored.

I should text Mack to invite him over for lunch. He should be back from the build site by now.

Me: Are you back yet? Want to come over for lunch?

I fill a glass with water from the jug in the fridge, gulp down half of it, and let a burp roar. It echoes off the walls and I giggle like a five-year-old boy.

Mack: I just got to Shaina's. We're heading to Rosie's diner in about twenty minutes. Join us. I'm sure she would love to see you.

Me: I don't want to intrude on your date.

Mack: Don't be ridiculous. Meet us!

Me: Do you think it'll be crowded?

Mack: It will be lunchtime so I imagine it will be.

I gulp the rest of the water. Eventually, people will get used to seeing us in public together … won't they?

Me: Okay, I'll meet you.

Mack: Excellent! Drive safely.

Me: You too!

I rush to throw my hair into a ponytail, slip into my light-weight pale blue dress and sandals, and then dig my tiny clutch purse from the box at the back of the walk-in closet I have yet to unpack.

I arrive before they do despite the sheets of rain that make it damn near impossible to see the road at times. I run into the restaurant and stop just inside. My hair is stuck to my face after the rain and whirlwind I just sprinted through. I do my best to put it back in order. Nobody gives me a sideways glance which has me at ease. Maybe they don't care that the town's harlot is in the room. Good!

Luckily, there's a table at the back of the restaurant where we'll less likely be ogled while we eat. I recognize the waitress to be Alicia, daughter of Larry and Wendy Gibson. I used to babysit her when she was seven. She smiles and addresses me by my name. We exchange pleasant greetings before I order a coffee and tell her I'm expecting guests.

She sets the mug of coffee in front of me just as Mack and Shaina arrive. Shaina wraps her arms around me and then quickly pulls back to give me a wet kiss on my lips. I scan the room for critics but no one's paying us any attention.

"I missed you so much!" she says as she slides onto the booth across the table from me.

"It's been a while, hasn't it?" I reply and wipe her burgundy lipstick off my lips.

"Goldilocks, you look beautiful as always." Mack gives me a quick peck on the lips before he sits beside his girlfriend.

It's strange but they don't look right together. Some couples suit one another; these two don't. It's not because she's Black and he's white; she's a city girl who wears lots of make-up, always has her hair styled—which is odd considering the weather outside. Unlike mine, her nails are long and painted, and she always wears fashionable clothing. She's fun and pretty, but high maintenance; not the kind of woman I would expect Mack to be interested in.

Mack's long hair fans over the flannel, grey and black plaid shirt he left unbuttoned to reveal a snug black t-shirt. He's usually in well-worn blue jeans that accentuate his thick thighs and tight ass, and I've only ever seen him in running shoes or hiking boots. He's a woodsman through and through.

The waitress takes their drink orders and scurries away. Shaina still seems overly excited to see me. "I'm so happy you called. It's always so great to see you." She leans forward and taps her nails on the menu. "So, what have you been up to lately?"

"I've been getting the house together, trying to figure out where things need to be situated. I just hung a bunch of pictures I got from the second-hand store. They'll do for now." She's put off from the mention of the second-hand store.

She relaxes her scrunched nose. "I'm sure they're lovely; vintage, as they say. We all have to start somewhere," she says while scanning the menu.

Her tone seemed condescending. She may very well feel more superior than me but it's rude to point it out.

The waitress brings their drinks and with a click of her pen, she's prepared to take our orders. Shaina fusses with her thick gold necklace when she asks to exchange a garden salad for a Caesar to go with her tuna-melt sandwich. When the waitress informs her of the price difference, she complains but still wants the exchange.

Mack rubs his hands together. "So, Patch and Bash met your friend, Lizzy." He smirks and waves his eyebrows. "I hear Patch is especially fond of her."

"He, ah…" I feel like I'm gossiping. "He *really* liked her."

Shaina looks annoyed. "Did Patch fuck a friend of yours?" I nod and she glares at Mack. "When did this happen and why am I only hearing about it now?" He shrugs as if to say he doesn't know.

To save him from her inquisition, I say, "It only happened a few days ago, and Mack's been at the site…" I pause when she purses her lips. I can't tell if she's angry, jealous, or anxious to hear more? I look at Mack who pays her no attention.

Mack leans forward. "He told me he wants to see her again. Said she challenged him, much like someone else I know." He squints his eyes at me. "He said you enjoyed watching them."

I simply smile innocently. He wants to hear the dirty details but I sip coffee to make him wait. I whisper so no one will overhear. "She rode him like he was a bucking bronco. Afterward, she thanked him, said it was fun, and then walked away as if she were done with him. His reaction was priceless. He's used to women fawning over him, especially after sex."

Mack grins widely and runs his fingers through his long hair. He's pleased that someone put Patch in his place. "He probably felt rejected."

Officer Grant Callan, an old high school acquaintance, enters and tips his head to let the water drip from his hat. He looks around and then advances toward us. He doesn't sit at the vacant bench before ours like I thought he would; he continues and stops beside Mack.

"Hello, Mack," he says and tips his hat toward me, then Shaina. "Goldilocks. Ma'am. It's been a while, hasn't it?" I nod and smile.

"Callan," Mack juts his hand out and the two greet one another. "How the hell are you? I haven't seen you since high school graduation."

It's strange to see Grant dressed in a cop's uniform. When we were teenagers, he was the biggest pot smoker in town. I don't know what happened for him to turn his life around the way he did, but the uniform suits him.

"You're probably right." He shifts his weight to the other leg. "One of these days I'm going to have to come over to see the new house. I hear it's really something to see."

Mack turns his face to look at the cop. "It's a great house. It's not spectacular but you'll like it." He looks at me.

"I love it and it is spectacular," I reply.

Grant takes off his hat to run his fingers through his thick red hair before he puts it back on. He glances at the officer that sat at the empty table, who's busy reading the menu. "Well, I don't want to interrupt your lunch," he pauses to shake his head. "I'll never forget that time we went to the quarry and you jumped but didn't get a running start and hit a few rocks on the way down. Shit, I thought you were a goner!"

Mack takes a sip of his soda. "I have a scar on my leg from that."

The cop laughs, "You should have had stitches."

"Nah!" Mack waves his hand. "It healed—took a while but it healed."

"Patch was so mad at you for that." He looks at me and then Shaina. "He chased Mack around the yard but he couldn't catch him. Even with a split leg and multiple scrapes and bruises, he was fast as hell."

"I ran faster scared than he did angry," Mack laughs.

Callan snickers and rests his hands on his hips. "Well, I'll never forget it." His shoulders lift and he presses his lips into a thin line. "All right," he says then pats the table. "Good seeing you. Give me a call some time." They shake hands. He nods toward us ladies. "Goldilocks. Ma'am."

Callan walks away and Shaina huffs and rolls her eyes.

"What's wrong with you?" Mack sighs heavily and picks up his menu and begins reading it. I hold my menu up but look over it to watch the show.

She turns her head to look him up and down while her lips twist. "Are you ashamed to have me as your girlfriend?"

He drops his menu and folds his hands over it. "What makes you think that?"

Her arms cross over her chest. "You didn't introduce me." Mack looks at me. "Goldilocks isn't going to answer for you?" she says with arrogance.

He shakes his head. "I didn't think about it, that's all." He snickers. "And no, I'm not ashamed of you. Not at all." He pecks a kiss on her lips and she seems to soften.

"All right, then. Don't do it again."

He places his hand over his heart. "I'll never not introduce you again."

Our conversation is casual as we eat; mostly we talk about the mansion being built that Mack designed.

The waitress takes our plates and sets the bill on the table. I pick it up but Mack yanks it from my fingers. He insists, "I'll take that."

"No! At least let me pay for my own," I argue.

He squares his shoulders and shakes his head. "Not going to happen!"

I point my finger at him. "Fine, but I'm getting it next time."

Shaina looks at her pinky fingernail with a frown. "You should know you can't argue with this man when it comes to paying for shit."

With my elbows resting on the table, I form a steeple with my fingers and rest my chin atop. "We don't often go out in public."

Mack reaches across the table and strokes my forearm. "No," he whispers and waves his brows over hooded eyes. "We find ways to entertain ourselves at home." He winks.

My face heats up. I meet Shaina's quirky smile. My eyes widen as my brows lift and I inhale deeply. "You know what he's like. He can be very entertaining."

"Mhm," she agrees. "It's true; he loves to shove his cock up the asses of willing women. And you're about as willing as they come." She grins, then nips at her fingernail.

"Hey, now!" Mack leans away from Shaina but turns to look at her. "Don't slut-shame! We don't do that. Besides, you have never denied having my cock deep inside your ass."

She rests her hand on his thigh. "I wasn't shaming her. I'm just as much of a slut as she is. I fuck you and your brothers just like she does."

She shocks me when she insinuates that she's presently fucking all of them including Bash. "Have you been with Bash lately?"

She shrugs one shoulder and waves her hand at me dismissively. "Don't you talk to your man?"

Mack can sense my irritation. His hand pats mine, which are folded on the table in front of me. "She hasn't been with Bash in a long time. We have no secrets in this family." He pauses and looks at Shaina. "Do we?"

She shrugs again. "No. No secrets."

He pats her shoulder then stands. "I'll be back." He struts toward the cash register and I nearly burst into laughter when two women in their forties stop their conversation and follow him with their eyes. They whisper and giggle.

"I'm not fucking your man," Shaina says, breaking the silence between us.

I sit back and fold my hands on my lap. "That's what Mack said."

"Since you freaked out when you found out he fucked me that one time, he won't touch me." She crosses her arms in front of her and rests her forearms on the table. "Pity because he's a great fuck. That man's cock had me screaming."

I hide my irritation as best I can. "He does have an exceptional cock."

She's glaring at me. "Listen," she whispers, then turns and sees Mack is still at the cash-out and is flirting with the cashier. "Since I can't touch your man, you can't touch mine."

"What?" I lean in, unsure if I heard her right. "Do you have a problem with me?"

Her shoulders lift. "Since you asked..." She sits tall but keeps her arms crossed over her chest. "I don't like it when you call Mack and he goes running. Until Bash wants to fuck me again, I think you should keep your hands to yourself."

"Oh, wow!" I pause to take a deep breath so I don't make a scene. I lean toward her with my clenched fists. I whisper, "If you have an issue with me and Mack, you should have said so right from the beginning." I sigh heavily. "I don't want to get into this here. We can discuss this another time and in a more suitable location."

I scan the other patrons who aren't paying us any attention. Mack is leaning on the counter while he slips his wallet into his back pocket. He's smiling at the woman and she's obviously smitten.

She leans back. "At least I know where my man is all the time."

My eyes shoot back to her smug face. "What the fuck does that mean? I don't need to know to keep tabs on Bash because I trust him."

She smirks. "Mhm."

"Why didn't you want to talk about this when Mack was sitting here? Are you afraid he'll dump you?"

She spits, "Fuck no! The man loves me."

I roll my eyes and decide to play dirty. "Did he actually tell you that? He tells me he loves me all the time." Her lips purse and her eyes shift. "I take that as a no."

Without another word—because I won that argument—I pick up my purse and weave through the tables toward Mack. He spots me and then winks at the cashier, who's flushed. She sees me and scurries away.

"I have to get going." He lifts his arm over my shoulder and pulls me in for a lengthy hug. "Thank you for lunch."

He eases his grip and kisses me before he releases me. "I'm glad you came." He looks over my shoulder at Shaina who's standing behind me. His bright blue eyes burn into mine. "Maybe we can meet up later? Dinner at the main house, perhaps." He lifts my hand and kisses the back of it.

"I'm not sure what Bash has planned if anything. One of us will call you," I say, then kiss him once more for good measure because I know it bothers her. "Love you."

"I love you, too, beauty," he whispers and runs his finger down my nose. "Drive safely."

I leave and say nothing else to her.

I'm huffing mad and regret not tossing my half-full glass of ice water in her face. I slam the car door and scream. When I attempt to throw my purse on the passenger's seat, some of its contents spill onto my lap and the floor. The strap is stuck in the door. I free it and slam it a second time and then growl as I grip the wheel and yank and push until my arms are tired.

Mack looks for my car as they're walking out. He waves so I smile and wave back. She waves, too. I ram the key in the ignition and start the engine.

I drive calmly despite my mood. How did this day veer so badly off course? It started off so well and then *her!* Should I tell Mack his girlfriend has staked her claim on him and wants me out of the picture? I know Mack to be a free spirit. If she holds him tightly, she'll lose him. I'll talk to him about it but I'll do it when we're alone.

Did Bash step out on me, as she insinuated? Is there another woman? What reason would he have to lie about something like that? He wouldn't. She's just trying to stir the pot; unless he's having sex with her but afraid to tell me because I got upset the last time. What if Mack doesn't know? I can't think like that.

Why am I doubting Bash?

He *has* been working a lot of hours, and he's distracted when he's home. Too often, I see him stare at the wall and deep in thought. When I ask, he says he's just thinking about his book.

CHAPTER ELEVEN

The four of us have dinner at the main house. Patch cooked his delicious rabbit stew. Even though there are times I could mention the conversation I had with Shaina, I don't. We're having such a great time, and I don't want to ruin it.

I brought a chocolate cheesecake with me for dessert and the guys praised me for it. It was a big cake but there's nothing left after they have seconds. I help Patch clean the kitchen while Bash and Mack sit on the deck with a beer and a cigar.

After he tells me about his worker having a near miss when they downed a tree earlier today, I beg him to be safe. He kisses my forehead.

"We're as careful as we can be," he says as he dries his hands on the dishtowel I'm using. "So," he pauses to bite his lip as he leans against the counter with his hands on his hips. "What's Lizzy been up to? I haven't heard from her."

A smile creeps onto my face. "She doesn't want to be in a relationship, so she probably won't call you." I hang the towel over the oven handle, slide my arms around his waist, and look up at him as he looks down his nose. "She does want to fuck you again."

His face lights up. "Well, that sounds like fun. When?"

"Look at you," I tease. "You're smitten with her."

"Maybe I am." His chin lifts and his hands rub my back. "She's funny, intelligent, fucking hot as a demon straight out of hell, and she fucks like a wild cat. Of course, I like her."

"And she challenged you," I say and step away from him. I do a little dance. "You like her! You like her! She's sexy and you like her!"

His eyebrows lower but he laughs. "You're so fucking weird." He takes a beer from the fridge and offers me one but

I turn it down and point to my glass of water. "But I love your weird."

We join the guys on the porch to share more laughs. A while later, Bash says, "Well, Goldie, it's getting late and you have to get up for work. We all know how much you love to sleep."

The brothers nod and chuckle.

"She's just getting her beauty sleep," Mack sticks up for me. I blow him a kiss as I stand.

Patch adds, "It's working, so who are we to criticize." He stands with his empty beer bottle and offers to take Bash's.

Mack waves his eyelashes and lifts his eyebrows to entice me with his boyish charm. "I'm going to kiss you." He pauses to gaze up and down my body. "Ready?"

I nod, and he springs from his chair, wraps an arm around my back and plants a sensual kiss on my lips, and then dips me. He's a lover of old movies and I think that's where he gets his tips for seduction.

After I'm righted, I glide over to Patch and brush my fingernails down his bare muscular forearm. He sets the empty bottles on the table. Before I can react, his strong hand is weaved in my hair and he's kissing me firmly. If Mack's kiss hadn't aroused me, this one sure as hell will do the trick. He releases me and immediately collects the bottles and heads into the house as if he didn't just make my pussy damp. I'm flushed and trembling.

I go inside and get my purse. As I'm heading to the kitchen, Patch steps in front of me. I hear the door open and Mack and Bash enter while they're laughing about something. Patch's palm glides along my jaw until it rests on the side of my neck. He leans in and presses his lips to the other side of my neck, and then breathes in my scent. He moans and kisses softly along my jaw to my lips. He leans back and looks into my eyes.

What is he thinking? I can't read him. The corner of his lip lifts. "I love you, Goldie."

I grimace. "Stop calling me Goldie. That's Bash's nickname for me." He chuckles as he walks over to Bash. They shake hands and bump chests.

Bash asks, "Patch, are you coming back to the house or staying here tonight?"

He replies, "I'm staying here. Mack and I are going to shoot the shit like brothers do." Patch grabs Mack in a headlock. "We might even get drunk."

I stomp my foot like a child. "I want to stay!"

With his arm wrapped around my shoulder, Bash looks down at me. "Not this time, Goldie. You have to work in the morning."

Mack wrestles with Patch and manages to slip from his grasp. He nearly knocks Patch on his ass in the process. Both men laugh like young boys.

Despite all the excitement and Patch ready to charge, Mack says, "Yeah, but *you* don't have to work tomorrow, little brother." Bash looks at me questioningly.

I roll my eyes. "Fine! Go ahead. I'll drive myself home." I pop my bottom lip out to exaggerate my pout.

Mack laughs. "Thank you, Goldie."

"I love you, Goldie," Patch says as Mack rushes him.

"Don't destroy the place before I get back," Bash says, then opens the door to usher me to my car. He opens the car door for me and we both cringe when we hear a kitchen chair topple.

I sit in the car and toss my purse on the passenger's seat. "Hey, I keep forgetting to ask you about someone, and since she just popped into my head again…"

"Who?"

"Sarah Joyeau." He closes my car door and I put the window down after I turn the key to auxiliary.

He rubs his forehead. "Yeah, she's a sore spot with us."

Curious, I ask, "Why's that? She seemed nice; a bit twitchy, but nice."

"Where did you meet her?" he asks as he places his hands on the roof.

"The place I bought the pictures from. She works there."

"Do you want the whole story?" I nod with wide eyes. "Mack started dating her. So, with her permission, we started fucking her." He clears his throat. "She started coming over when she knew I'd be home alone. It quickly became apparent that she favored me sexually. As you can imagine, Mack wasn't thrilled. After a while, she refused to spend any time alone with Patch because she said he scared her."

He bends down to lean his elbows on the driver's door. "But the final straw was when she told Mack she didn't want him anymore because she fell in love with me." He taps his fingers on the door.

"Yeah, she said you told her your heart belonged to someone else." I tilt my head like I'm an overzealous teenager. "Do tell who?"

He furrows his brow. "Seriously? You don't know?" I shake my head. "You! My heart was yours the first time I set eyes on you, way back when girls were still yucky."

My heart melts and I can't think of anything to say that would do justice to his confession. He leans in, looks lovingly into my eyes, and kisses me softly. If I wasn't already in love with him, that kiss would have me swooning.

"Does that happen a lot?" I ask. "Do women start dating one of you but lean more toward another?"

He drops his head and clears his throat. "From time to time." He pauses. "It happened with you, too; well, sort of."

I jerk my head and look at him, shocked and confused. "What are you talking about?"

He rubs his chin and looks everywhere but at me. "You're with me and you love me, but you're in love with Patch, too." He shrugs. "Like I said, it happens."

What the fuck do I say? He's right; I love Patch. Yes, I'm in love with both of them and I never thought it possible. If I had to choose, would I choose Bash? Yes, I'm sure I would.

"I love you! You know I love you. I mean, I do—"

"Listen," he interrupts, then pauses to clear his throat. "I'm happy that you love Patch and Mack. I'm okay with you being in love with Patch. I know you love me, too. Hopefully more than him. But if not, never tell me. Okay?"

"I do. I'm not—" I shake my head and for whatever unknown reason, maybe deep-rooted guilt, I can't maintain eye contact. "I'm … I love you both."

"Yeah," he smiles but the corners of his eyes don't crease. "I know. It's good."

Bash leans in and kisses me with a tenderness that has me wishing I could wrap myself around him. He pats the door as he steps back.

He points at me and insists, "Text me when you get home and the doors are locked."

"I will. Now go play with your brothers." I drive away and watch him through the rear-view mirror until the driveway arches. This conversation might need more discussion.

***

After a long, hot shower, I blow dry my hair and expect he'll be home soon.

Did I leave with a huge question mark between us? I keep running the conversation through my head. Does he feel pushed aside? If he can't be honest about his feelings this early in our relationship, how can we possibly survive a full year let alone a lifetime?

At 12:30, he's still not home. I close my book and snuggle under the covers.

I startle awake when something thuds in the living room. My ears strain and my heart pounds. I hear another thump and boots shuffle on the hardwood floor. Two men shush each other but fail to muffle their laughter. It's Bash and Mack, and they're drunk.

It's 2:30! Should I be angry? The guys like to drink but I've never seen any of them full-on drunk. Happy, yes. Drunk, no.

"Shh, you'll wake her," one voice whispers.

"We should wake her and maybe we can…" the other says but stops to sing some porn music. I laugh but fight to keep quiet. "We could rock her world because we know how to, and we can, we can do it."

I think that's Bash's voice and he's sloshed.

I'm sure their alcohol-induced limp dicks would overrule any desire they may have to rock my world. I clamp my lips between my teeth to prevent my laughter from being heard. What a couple of clowns!

Mack whispers. "Okay, now!" Laughter. "Now sneak in there and—" More laughter from both men. "And slide in really quiet-like." Both giggle like happy drunk men.

"Yeah, I'm gonna! Yeah."

"Just, you gotta be, like, um…" More giggles and then both men shush each other rather loudly. "Be very quiet. Like a quiet tiptoeing mouse. Like that quiet. Okay?"

"Yeah! What? You don't think I'm quiet? I'm a—I can be a quiet guy. Like, I'm a mouse. A really big fucking mouse!"

Loud laughter, then shushes.

I'm about to burst. This is hysterical! Tears spill from the corners of my eyes and onto my pillow. My hands cover my mouth to hold in my laughter.

"Hey, middle brother?"

"What's up, baby brother?" Mack whispers and then laughs.

Bash says, almost low enough to be a whisper, but not quite, "You're my favorite brother because you didn't fall in love with my Goldie."

"Nah, man! Come on! I am in lo—I mean, I love her too, but like, um, I mean, there's Shaina, but I don't think I love her."

I hear a thump and a shush followed by another thump.

92

Mack says, "Dude, you're too loud."

"Well, I can't go to bed with my boots on."

The door slowly opens wide, allowing their hushed banter into the room unobstructed. It's like their drunken stupor had them believing it was a magical door that kept out all sound. There's a distant sound of footsteps in the living room, and then the front door shuts.

Bash is quiet aside from his clothing landing on the floor as he strips. The bed jerks and he stifles a laugh. The covers lift and he slides in up against my back and flops his arm over my waist. He pulls me so my butt presses against his belly. He reeks of beer and whiskey.

His whisper is faint, but I'm sure it's louder than he hoped it to be. "I love you, my Goldie girl, and I've never been more afraid."

In a few seconds, he's snoring, and I'm left to wonder why loving me scares him.

CHAPTER TWELVE

I wake to the scent of bacon cooking. My arm stretches to the other side of the bed in search of the warm body who passed out next to me, but he's not here. I stuff my face in his pillow and breathe in his scent. A waft of his cologne lingers.

How the hell is he up and able to make breakfast when he's likely still drunk?

Plates click together, and that's the signal I should get up. He'll soon come to fetch me and tease me for being a late sleeper, even though it's only 7:30am. All three boys wake before 6am every day, no matter what. They referred to me as Rumpelstiltskin for a week after I slept past 8:30am.

The door slowly opens with whisper silence. I quickly fling my legs over the edge of the bed and raise my arms over my head to stretch as my jaw gapes from a lengthy yawn.

"You didn't sleep well last night?" he says as more of a question.

I reply, "It's hard to sleep next to someone who snored as loudly as you did."

He carries in a full tray: two plates full of food, two coffee mugs, a bowl of fruit, and a small vase that holds a fat white rose. "Get back in bed. You're ruining the whole breakfast in bed stereotypical romantic moment."

"Sorry, I was unaware of the protocol for etiquette pertaining to the breakfast in bed scenario. I'll study up on the acceptable reactions for future loving or apologetic gestures."

He grimaces. "Sorry about snoring."

My eyes lock on the beautiful pink-tipped white rose. "Where'd you get this? It's too early for the flower shops to be open."

He sits on his side of the bed, holds up the tray, and gestures to its legs. "Would you be so kind?"

I adjust them and he sets it between us. As he tries to find a level spot amid the tousled comforter, I pick up the rose and stick it under my nose. My eyes close as I sniff in until my lungs are full.

I'm reminded of a hot summer day when I was a child. I sat among the rose bushes and Mom was taking pictures. I was maybe three-years-old. My father told me to look at her, to smile, and not to squint. But the sun peeked under the brim of my hat when I'd look up. Mom warned me about the thorns and it scared me. I stood up and fell. I remember the red blood on the white petals. I open my palm to admire the scar left from a thorn.

"Do you like it?" His voice pulls me back from my memory.

I close my eyes, and the edges of my lips lift. I moan my approval and open my eyes just as he tucks a tress of tangled hair behind my ear.

I breathe in the rose's scent one more time. "I'm keeping it forever," I say as I set it back on the tray.

"I woke up and you were having a bad dream," he says with a questioning expression. "Want to talk about it?"

"I don't remember it. Why didn't you wake me?"

He quickly looks down at the tray. "Here, eat. It'll help give your sleepy ass some energy," he teases and hands me a plate and fork. He leans against the headrest with a plate of his own.

I ask, "Was I saying anything?"

His eyes don't meet mine. He shoves food around his plate before he stabs a chunk of egg and stuffs it in his mouth. He glances at my plate as he chews.

He waves his fork. "Eat. It's good for you," he says between chews.

"You're being evasive." I set the plate on my lap. "Did I say something you didn't like?"

He sets his fork on his plate but takes too long to swallow the bite of egg. "Yes, you were mumbling." His eyes meet mine. "Specifically, you were saying Patch's name, a lot. The words *I love you* came up more than once." He shrugs, then shoves a whole piece of bacon in his mouth.

"I'm sorry. I was asleep. I don't remember the dream. I have no control over what I—" I stop talking when he smiles and winks.

He covers his mouth. "I know you love him, and I'm happy you do." He pauses to chew and swallow. "The relationship you have with him is different than it is with me. I understand that. Even though we're brothers, Patch and I are not the same. I wouldn't expect your experiences with him to parallel ours." He runs his fingers down my cheek. His eyes plead with me. "Just, please, let me love you more."

My heart aches. I slice through my egg with my fork and stab it. "I heard what you said when you got into bed last night." I shove the fork in my mouth and moan at how delicious it tastes.

He nods and looks back at his plate. "I figured as much. Sorry, I was drunk. People say things when they're drunk and—"

"People tend to say what they mean when they've lost their inhibitions from an alcohol-induced stupor." I stab another chunk of egg. "And don't worry. I love you and I'm not going anywhere."

"I know. But," he pauses to clear his throat. He fiddles with his fork. "You had a lot of time alone with Patch while I was at school. Mack was away at the build more often than he was home. Patch took great care of you, so of course, you love him. I'm happy you do, I really am. I gave you my heart with no regrets."

He tips his head back against the headrest and looks at me. "Much like you never having been in a sexually explorative relationship, I've never given my heart to anyone before. This

Pebbles Lacasse

is new territory for me. As much as I don't want to admit it …
it scares me."

He continues to eat as if he didn't just beg me not to tear
him to pieces. Nothing more is said about it. I eat more than
my share before I shower and get ready for work while he
makes the bed and tidies the kitchen.

I love him. I really, really love him. What the fuck is wrong
with me?

Why won't I let Patch fall to the wayside and focus all of
my energy on Bash, which is what I've wanted since the day
we met back in grade school? He said he loves to share me
with his brothers. Maybe I should stop reading so much into
it and freely love them all, just differently, as Bash suggested.

***

They're short-staffed in the surgical preparation wing so
Laura, my supervisor, has me work there for the day. I have
the least amount of seniority and expect to be shuffled around
but I prefer to be in the operating room.

An elderly, fragile woman aided with a cane slowly makes
her way toward the check-in desk where I sit.

"Hello," I say with a welcoming smile.

She returns the gesture, and her wrinkles deepen. "Hello.
Is this where I need to check in?"

"If you're here for day surgery, you're in the right place."
I point to the chair next to the desk. "Please, have a seat, and
let me get some information from you."

She tells me her name is Marianna Colt, and she was born
on November 3, 1935.

I take a moment to study her face and then lie to her. "You
don't look a day over sixty-five."

She bursts into laughter. "Oh, dear! I appreciate that but
I'm old, not blind." She pats my hand. "You're a young, pretty
girl. Do you have a man in your life?"

Actually, I have three!

"Yes, I do."

She smiles as grandmothers do. "Good! Marry the man and have lots of sex. It'll keep you young and put a bounce in your step."

I nod but quickly change the subject. "Looks like you're scheduled for a minor procedure. I'll have to give you an I.V."

She shrugs as though she hasn't a care in the world. I prepare the smallest needle we have and try to find a viable vein which isn't easy in a woman of her age. After two failed attempts, the woman's obviously irritated.

"What's your name, dear?" she asks.

"Goldilocks," I say while I search for a worthy vein. I've never had to poke three times, and I'm beginning to doubt myself.

She's quiet which is unlike her. I look at her to make sure she isn't about to pass out. She's expressionless as she studies my face. I press the button on the blood pressure monitor and she rolls her eyes, irritated that the cuff will soon squeeze her arm for the third time.

She says, "I suppose telling *you* to have lots of sex wasn't warranted. You're the woman living with those hoodlums; the Bear boys." She points her shaky finger at me. "I've heard all about you."

Has all the blood left my face? I think it has. Back in her day, I would have been considered a societal leper and cast out of town as a Jezebel and forever disrespected.

"Is there another nurse who can tend to me?" She glances down the hall with hopes a nurse will magically appear.

I clear my throat and release the pressure cuff before I pick up the phone. I call my supervisor, Laura.

The lull of uncomfortable silence fills the room for several minutes before the familiar heavyset woman with the brown hair twisted into a bun stomps around the corner wearing a friendly smile.

"Hello," Laura says with a strong southern accent. "Goldilocks, how can I help?"

Before I can explain, the woman speaks. "I don't want this harlot poking me again. She tried twice already and well—" Her tone is demeaning. She leans closer to Laura and fails in her attempt to whisper. "She's obviously unqualified to work with someone my age. Besides, how can I be sure she doesn't have one of those new diseases she might give me?"

Laura scratches her head. I shake my head and nervously chew on my cuticle. She nods to suggest I leave. I'm grateful for the dismissal.

I barely make it to the employee restroom before I erupt into a crying fit. How can someone be so rude? I know she's elderly but that doesn't give her the right to be an asshole. My personal life is my own. Isn't it?

After ten minutes and a splash of cold water on my face, I'm composed. I'm relieved to see a different woman seated just down the hall. I force a smile and wave her over.

The rest of my shift was uneventful. I doubt I could have survived another difficult patient. But before I go, I check in with Laura to apologize for earlier. When I tap on her door frame, she calls me into her office and waves her hand for me to close the door.

"Goldilocks, please don't think I'm passing judgment on your lifestyle because I'm not. My religion has taught me that it's not my place to judge anyone. I am, however, going to suggest you keep your personal life personal. In other words, don't bring your drama into my department."

Thankfully, she doesn't raise her voice. With a nod, I reach for the door handle.

"Goldilocks," she calls to me and waits until I look at her. "If you ever need to talk, I'm a good listener and I don't flap my gums. My door is always open." She smiles and it's believable.

"Thanks. I'll keep that in mind." I hastily retreat.

I'm torn between tears, pity, and a raging anger by the time I get to my car. I start the engine and push the buttons to drop the windows.

Before I drive, I call Mom and Dad's house. Although my dad said he'd try to come to grips with my relationship with the Bear brothers, he hasn't given much effort. I've invited them over for dinner a few times but there's always an excuse why Dad can't make it. Mom comes over often but Dad has visited only once and didn't stay an hour.

The ringer sounds loud in my small car. It rings three times before someone answers.

"Hello?" It's more a question than a greeting. "Hello? Mom?" More silence. "Dad?"

"Mom's not home." Dad's voice is vacant of emotion. "Do you need something?"

"Um, no," I reply. "I was just looking to chat with Mom. I had an awful day at work. This one patient gave me a hard time and—"

"Listen, Goldilocks, Mom isn't home and I'm on my way out. I can write her a note or you can call her cell phone. Although, I doubt she'll answer; she's at the legion jarring pickles with the ladies."

"Oh, right." I recall the conversation where she invited me to join her. "Okay, I'll try her later."

"Good-bye, Goldilocks."

He hangs up quickly. My dad didn't give ten minutes of his time to listen to his daughter talk about her shitty day at work. He's a tough-hearted man. We used to chat for hours but that was before I gave myself to the town's evil spawn.

When I stopped at a light, I look for Lizzy's address in my phone. If her car's there, I'll stop. She always lifts my mood and I could use that right about now.

I rap at the screen door and see her rush toward me. "Hey, hey!" She opens the door. "Come on in! I was just burning cookies. I mean, baking cookies." She giggles.

The smell of burnt food stings my nostrils. She wasn't kidding when she said she was burning cookies. I follow her through the living room. It could use some upgrades. The dining room as well. The old table hasn't weathered the years well enough to be referred to as vintage.

We enter the kitchen through a small archway and the smell intensifies. A wood-framed window above the sink is propped open with a wooden ladle. The back door is held wide open by an old metal-framed kitchen chair with rips in the plastic backrest and seat.

She points to a tray of blackened cookies. "Like I said." She pulls out a chair that looks just as worn as the other. "Have a seat. So, what brings you here?"

While we talk, I watch her scrape the burnt pucks from the metal sheet and then plop fresh balls of dough in four rows of three. She sets them in the oven and adjusts the timer shaped like an egg.

"I had an awful day," I pout.

She wrestles the chair from the door then sits kitty-corner to me. "Of course, you did!" She gloats, "I wasn't there to keep you entertained."

"Well, that's one reason," I say with a nod.

"What happened?"

I roll my eyes and take a deep breath. "I was in receiving today," I say and she scrunches her face to show her distaste for the position. "Some old woman… She was fine with letting me try a third time for her I.V. but refused after I told her my name. She recognized me as being the sinner living with three men."

"Did it cross your mind that she didn't want you to stab and miss a third time? Maybe it had nothing to do with you personally."

I lean back and the chair wobbles on its uneven legs. "No, she wasn't coy about it. She even told Laura that she thought I might give her a disease. It was humiliating! I cried in the bathroom." I shake my head and raise my palms. "It wasn't the first time I've been degraded and it won't be the last."

"Eventually, you'll get used to it. Either that," she leans in and whispers, "or you'll have to start telling people to fuck off."

"I heard that!" A red-haired woman strolls in from the other room. She dons a fluffy purple robe and a smile. Her red nose and droopy eyes are evidence she doesn't feel well. "A lady doesn't swear," she pauses. "In public."

Lizzy lowers her face but not her eyes. "We're not in public."

"Oh, then go ahead." The woman, who's likely her mother, pats her on the shoulder before she notices me. "I'm sorry. I'm not dressed for company." She fusses with her robe. "I'd shake your hand but you'll appreciate it more if I don't. I'm sick." She lifts her hand to reveal a crumpled tissue.

Lizzy waves her hand between us. "Mom, this is Goldilocks. Goldilocks—Ginger, AKA my mother."

The woman's smile drops quickly and what little color she had in her cheeks has washed away, leaving her very pale. It suddenly dawns on me where I've heard that name before. Ginger is the woman who saw me bound to a tree and getting fucked by all three brothers in the woods.

She told one person and it spread like wildfire. Soon, the whole town knew about it. Worst was my parents heard, which is why my dad has been so short with me. Mom accepted my choice to be with them but Dad just can't. Because of her big mouth, I went from being known as the good girl who does everything right to a disgrace who spreads her legs for three brothers in the most deplorable ways.

She nearly ruined my life. If the guys weren't there to support me through all of that, I would have left town and never returned. The look on her face carries fear, embarrassment, and a plea for forgiveness. She waits for me to react.

Lizzy looks from her mom to me and back. "What's going on?"

As if snapped out of a trance, I look at a curious Lizzy and wonder how she doesn't know what her mother did. "Nothing. I thought I recognized her name."

Lizzy hops up to look in the oven at the cookies. "She works at the Mill Street bank. You probably saw her there."

"It's nice to meet you," I say to the short, thin woman.

She looks relieved that I haven't shoved my fist down her throat. "And you."

She reaches in the newer stainless-steel refrigerator to collect a bottle of orange juice, then retreats back to where she originated after she steals another wide-eyed glance at me. I want to punch her in the face and scream humiliating things at her so she can have a taste of how much she hurt me, but it won't fix anything. The truth about the brothers and me would have come out eventually. I would have preferred it to happen on my terms and with a bit more discretion.

I stand and the chair squeaks. "I should go."

Lizzy opens the oven and glares at me while she slips on an oven mitt. "You just got here!" She removes the tray of cookies which are baked to perfection. "At least stay for some cookies."

I sit back down and her little dance proves her excitement. A cookie drops from the tray, halting her dance moves. She pouts as if mourning its death and I laugh.

By the time I leave, I've eaten three delicious cookies and had a few laughs. We discussed what we could about our secrets but with her mom in the next room, we had to keep the conversation to more appropriate topics. Although she's put me in a much better mood, I know my woes will continue to haunt me.

***

Bash's truck isn't home when I arrive. With my forehead resting on the steering wheel, I turn the key to stall the engine. My arms hug the wheel and turn my head to look down at the river. The heavy downpours we've had over the past week have it rushing past.

After I lock my purse in the car, I head down the path toward my favorite place; the rock. Strangely, I doubted it would be there since my day has been shit. I roll my eyes at the ridiculous thought. It's a boulder. Boulders rarely move.

I stretch out on my tummy so I can watch the water rush past while the minnows huddle in the shallows to remain protected from predators. I feel akin to the minnows as I rest on this rock and hide from those who would cause me pain.

The sun is warm on my back, soothing, exactly what I need to ease tense muscles. The low-hanging sun reflects off the tiny waves like millions of sparkling diamonds. It's sedating.

CHAPTER THIRTEEN

"Goldie."

I'm annoyed.

"Goldilocks! Goldie…"

I jolt awake. Judging by the pain in my lower back and the darkness that surrounds me, I fell asleep on the rock some time ago. How long was I asleep?

"Goldilocks!"

Is that Patches voice?

"Goldie…" Bash? "Baby, where are you?"

"Guys?" I yell but my voice is hoarse and scratchy. I clear my throat and yell again as I peel myself off the rock with a groan. I stretch my arms over my head and bend to the left, then the right. "I'm here!"

"I hear her!" Patch yells.

He's close but I can't see him through the ebony shadows cast down from the trees. His boots thump the ground as he rushes toward me, but from which direction? I turn just in time for him to wrap his arms around me and hold me in a hug that's way too tight and I can feel him shake.

I squirm and he releases me but holds my shoulders to assess me for injury.

"I'm fine," I say after he turns me so the moon's light will void the shadows. "Seriously, I'm okay."

"What the fuck, Goldilocks? You scared me." He corrects, "You scared *us*."

"Sorry. I had a shit day at work and came here to decompress. I fell asleep so mission accomplished." I joke but he doesn't see the humor in the situation.

He picks me up wedding style and stares down at my face. "Don't fucking scare me like that again." His tone is threatening but I hear the fear behind the words and that hurts me more than anything. He carries me down the path.

"I'm capable of walking on my own. I'm not injured."

He huffs. "I don't care. I'm not ready to let you go."

"Did you think I ran away?" I joke and struggle against his grip. "Seriously, put me down!"

Patch sets me on my feet just as Bash storms toward us. You'd think I was gone for a week by how hard he hugs me.

"Dammit, Goldie," Bash hisses. "Your purse and phone were in your car and it was locked. You were nowhere! Fuck, Goldie!" His hands cradle my face. I must look annoyed because his head tilts and he speaks calmly. "Forgive us, we were scared for you. We thought something happened."

Okay, so my workday was shit and the woman was rude, but the love these men have for me can't be denied. They love me and I them.

Patch looks at the rock and rubs his chin. "Why were you out here sleeping on a rock?"

Bash holds my hand on the walk back to our house. Patch strolls silently behind as I tell them about the woman who upset me and how I met Ginger but kept a cool head. They were proud of me for that.

Will I ever get used to the stares, whispers, rumors, and blatant insults? Will it always be so hard or will our relationship eventually become old news where nobody cares anymore?

When we get back to the house, Bash hands me a glass of water and a granola bar. "Eat. Drink. Later, I'm going to fuck you so hard! I'm angry because you scared me and I need to work through that."

I laugh and stretch my back again. "You won't hear me argue."

He continues, "Eat. Drink. We have to go."

"Go? Go where?" I shake my head and toss the bar on the table. "I just got home and my back aches. The only place I'm going is in a bathtub filled with steaming hot water."

Patch, who stands beside the open front door, says, "Mack's in the hospital."

"What? Why? What happened? Oh, my God! Is he going to be okay?"

Panic! Fear!

Bash grips my shoulders and looks into my eyes. "He's going to be okay. He's been hurt worse. He took the bike out knowing the roads might still be slick from the rain this morning. He wiped out but he wore a helmet and his leathers so there's no road rash."

"Okay, but..." My words fall away.

Bash brushes hair off my cheek and cups my chin. "He'll be fine in a few weeks. We have to go." He tries to smile but I can see the concern in his eyes. He looks at Patch who's rocking from leg to leg. "He'll be so pissed about the bike having to go back in the shop."

"What?" I shake my head. "No fucking way is he getting back on that bike! One accident, okay. Two and there's a curse on that bike. It's gone! I will burn that fucking thing before I let him ride it again!"

Patch laughs and I turn to glare at him. "You'll have to take that up with him, little lady. He won't take too kindly to your suggestion."

I grab my purse and rush to the door. "It's not a suggestion!" I run past him and toss my car keys to Bash. "My car's faster."

A typical half-hour drive to the hospital took only ten minutes with Bash behind the wheel. The nurse won't tell us where he is. Instead, she directs us to a waiting room.

My heart pounds rapidly and I feel faint. I sit and my leg bounces to expel some of my nervous energy. Patch sits beside me and takes my hand. Is he looking for comfort or is this for my benefit? His hand still shakes. Bash paces but stops to look down the hall each time he passes the doorway.

The half-hour wait drags. Finally, a nurse comes. We all stand in anticipation and our hearts pound wildly.

"Are you Mack Bear's family?" he asks and we all nod. The tall, forty-something man puts his hands on his waist. "If you want to see him, follow me."

He leads us down the hall, around the corner, and down another hall before we enter a dimmed room. Mack is lying on the gurney with his hand on his forehead, the other arm propped on pillows.

He sees us and smiles but his eyes dance back and forth. "Sorry, I'm dizzy." He groans in frustration. "Quit moving, will you?" he jokes.

Patch in his typical fatherly tone, says, "So, you still have your sense of humor. That's a good sign. Now quit joking around. I'm pissed at you."

"Give me a break; I'm damaged," Mack smiles wide with his eyes barely open.

Bash stands on the other side of the bed and sizes him up. "Damn, brother, did you flip through the air and land on your face because you're fucking ugly! No! Wait! That's how you always look."

They chat while I attempt to straighten his matted hair but it's stiff. It's now that I see the line of stitches on his neck. My stomach leaps into my throat. I'm a nurse! This shouldn't bother me but it does. A slice like that could have killed him.

My words are faint. "Your neck…"

Bash and Patch groan and lean in for a better look while they wear disgusted expressions.

He snickers. "It could have been worse."

I snap at him. "Yes, you could have bled out."

He reaches over his belly so I take his hand which is scraped along the top. I try not to touch the wound. "I'm okay." He sighs. "Beauty, don't worry. Fuck, you're pretty! She's fucking gorgeous, isn't she?"

"Do they have you on pain killers?" Patch asks.

Mack snickers and raises his eyebrows. "Fuck, yeah! I'm floating, man. I asked if I can take some of this shit home but they said no. I'm still working on the nurse with the red top. I think I can sway her." He laughs hard, grimaces, and releases my hand to hold his ribs.

I wet some paper towels and start wiping the blood from his hair while Mack tells us how the bike started fishtailing and hit the loose gravel. He was thrown and landed on the other side of the small ditch, on a dead tree.

He said it hurt right away and there were a few minutes when he couldn't catch his breath. He thought his ribs were busted and puncturing his lungs. He said his life flashed before his eyes and all he saw was me beneath him while he slid into my ass that first time. Of course, he smiles at me and waves his brows.

"You're such a damn flirt," I whisper and twist my mouth.

"I love you, Goldie. You know that, right, baby?" Mack hooks his finger in the collar of my shirt when I bend over to look for any blood that I may have missed. He looks down my shirt. "You have the prettiest titties. Do you know that?"

A tall doctor I recognize but haven't been formally introduced to, walks in holding an iPad at his waist. He stops at the door when he sees all of us in the tiny room. He sees Mack's looking down my shirt while I argue with him to let go. He's kind enough to look away.

"Hey, doc! This is my family; my brothers and *our girlfriend*, Goldilocks." He sings "our girlfriend." Either Mack doesn't realize he just outed us or he doesn't care.

Patch and Bash try to get him to shut up but their efforts are futile. I hope the doctor doesn't recognize me and tries discussing it when I'm working. But he looks at me and nods as if we're old friends. Patch shakes his hand then Bash rounds the bed to greet him.

Damn this day!

Bash continues. "I was just saying how perfect her nipples are because they stiffen like pencil erasers. I could suck on them all day and never get bored."

The doctor pinches his lips together to ward off a grin. He looks at me and blinks several times before he looks down at his tablet.

"He was conscious when he arrived but he has a slight concussion. Other than some dizziness, he should be fine." I meet his tired eyes and he asks, "Are you his girlfriend?" I look at Bash and he nods so I confirm it. "You're a nurse?" I nod again. "I thought I recognized you."

I smile and try to think of something to say, but it's Patch that asks a question. "And his other injuries?"

The doctor clears his throat. "He broke his Ulna but it's still aligned so he won't require surgery. He has a fractured Clavicle, bruised Scapula, and some bruised ribs. He'll have to support his arm with a sling. Unfortunately, the paramedics said he landed in a dead tree and was cut up by some branches. He has some stitches in his neck. He's lucky it wasn't deeper."

Bash sighs and asks, "He'll be okay then?"

The doctor nods. "He'll be sore for a while but he'll recover. With a head injury, you'll need to wake him every hour to make sure he's coherent."

Patch pats the man on the shoulder and offers him his hand. "Thanks, doc."

The nurse comes in with bandages and sets them beside him before he gets some gloves. He bandages while I watch.

The doctor shakes Patch's hand then gives him a prescription. "You can take him home after his neck is bandaged. Fill this prescription downstairs before you leave." Bash leans in and shakes the doctor's hand and thanks him to which the doctor nods. "At eleven o'clock give him two tablets; they'll help with the pain. Tomorrow morning, he can start with one pill every six hours as needed. There's enough to get him through three days. He should be fine with acetaminophen after that."

I push past Patch. "Can I see the x-rays?" The doctor looks at me wide-eyed. "I'll be caring for Mack when we get him home so I'd like to know the extent of the injuries."

He brings the x-rays up on his tablet to show me. The nurse finishes. Bash helps Mack sit up while Patch takes a cut and bloody shirt from the bag of the clothes he wore when the paramedics brought him in. He cusses and stuffs it back in the bag, unbuttons his red checkered fleece shirt, and takes it off.

He's wearing a simple white t-shirt beneath and it's snug-fitting, which emphasizes his muscles. I notice the doctor check him out with a sideways glance while the guys help Mack dress. Occasionally, Mack cusses louder than what's appropriate in a hospital setting.

We drive much slower on the way home. Mack lies across the backseat with his head on my lap. I'm doing the best I can to hold his casted arm still but the potholes in the road make that a challenge.

We insist he eat a sandwich before we put him to bed. He falls asleep right away. He can thank the drugs for that. After his arm is propped up on pillows, the guys leave the room and shut the light out.

"Goldie?" Bash calls to me.

I whisper, "Give me a minute."

I lift Mack's head to free his hair from beneath his shoulder and it wakes him. "Hi, beauty. Don't be mad at me."

"I'm not angry. You're going to be fine, but your motorcycling days are over."

"Do I have a say in that?" he asks. I sternly shake my head. "Fine, I'll sell it."

"Thank you," I whisper, then lean in and kiss him. "How's your pain?"

"I'm okay." His eyelids seem heavy. "Did anyone call Shaina? She might like to know."

I tuck my hair behind my ear. "Yeah, I did. She's working; said she'll call you tomorrow."

He frowns. "Did she seem at all concerned?"

"Yeah," I say, but recall how cold she seemed when I talked to her. Maybe it was just because I was the one to call her. If it had been anyone else, she might have been more receptive. "She was working and could hardly hear me over the music. She'll call tomorrow."

His eyes close and his whisper is faint. "I love you."

"I love you, too."

CHAPTER FOURTEEN

I offer to stay at the main house in case Mack needs anything through the night and to wake him every hour, but Patch insists he'll tend to him.

When Bash and I get home, I fill the tub with hot water and swap my work clothes for a robe. I pour a glass of pinot grigio, illuminate the bathroom with the flicker of a candle flame, and then slip my weary body into the hot bath. My back still aches from lying on that huge rock. I used to love sleeping on it but there are consequences now that I'm a grown woman.

Bash taps on the door. "Can I come in?"

"Of course."

He closes the door behind him to hold the heat in the room. I wave for him to come in with me. He takes off his shirt as he kneels beside the tub. He dunks the sponge, then holds it over my left shoulder to allow the water to warm my exposed skin as it drains.

"I've been a bit off lately," he says. I shake my head but he insists. "Yes, I have. Please know I love that you enjoy my brothers. We've always shared everything and it's never bothered me." He pauses. "But I've never been in a steady relationship with someone I cared this much about, and I'm afraid to lose you. I want to be with you forever. I want you to carry my babies if you choose to, and I want to grow old with you."

"I want that, too. All of it." I insist he joins me.

He strips and slips in behind me. I rest against him. After he uses the sponge to dribble water on my chest, he lets it float and wraps his arms around my shoulders. We enjoy the silence, each of us lost in our own thoughts. I wonder if he thinks the same thoughts as me. The water has cooled and my fingers are wrinkled, so I sit up and pull the plug.

I stand and reach for my towel but he takes it from me, then helps me out of the tub. He dries every inch of me. I watch him dry himself and how his muscles flex through such a mundane task. He hangs the towels and takes my hand.

He stops halfway to the bed and spins us like a dancing couple. He weaves his fingers in my hair and pulls until my head tilts so his lips meet mine. His kiss is delicate, contradicting the tension he inflicts on my scalp.

Bash releases my hair and spins me again but stops me when I face away from him at the end of the bed. I giggle like a schoolgirl with a crush. He pushes on my upper back until I bend over the bed and he has my chest pinned to the comforter.

His fingers glide down between my ass cheeks and further until they're between my saturated pussy lips. They leave me and he moans. "You taste so fucking good, Goldie." His wet fingers glide between my folds.

In one swift movement, he's buried deep inside of me. The shock of his size has me unable to breathe. He holds still. With conviction, he says, "I said I was going to fuck you hard."

His hips pound against my rear, over and over until I'm drenched in sweat and gripping the comforter. I couldn't say my name if he insisted upon it.

Bash breathes fast as he wraps his hand around my bicep and pulls me off the bed, then flips me onto my back. He pushes my thighs up to my chest. His mouth envelops my dripping wet vagina.

Holy hell!

My pussy spasms with each flick of his tongue as he urges me closer to the most wonderful orgasm a woman can have—clitoral. My arms stretch out to my sides and grasp a fistful of the comforter. I have to hold myself down otherwise I'm sure I'd float away. I'm light, so damn light like I'm not made of flesh and bone but of only a soul.

Have I left my body? No, the physical pleasure is too great.

I spin and float as I fall into darkness. My clitoris is all of me and he licks every bit. He sucks and I let go—let go of every thought, every fear, everything that makes me *me*. I just am, and for a moment, I am unrecoverable.

I'm spun like a ragdoll onto my tummy with no help from me. I can't move, still lost in my euphoria. He straddles the back of my thighs and aims the head of his cock and pushes forward. Despite the tight spasms of my orgasmic walls, he slides right in and pushes my mind even further from reality.

His legs stretch alongside mine and hold my thighs together. With his forearms slid beneath my armpits, I pull my arms in to hug his. My fingers weave into his and hold on. His weight pins me to the bed.

He glides his cock into my pussy in a steady rhythm. My thoughts slowly return but not enough to stop myself from moaning each time he sinks into me. He pants against my shoulder.

I tense; I want more. There's pain on my shoulder but I give it no concern. I bounce under his powerful thrusts. I'm unable to think, move, or stop myself from grunting like a wild animal on the verge of its death—pure ecstasy.

Bash cries out. "You're mine! You're fucking mine!"

His lengthy scream signals the end of all things wonderful. He collapses beside me and I suddenly feel lonely, cold, and wrought with emotion.

I haven't moved; can't move, don't want to move. Tears gush onto the comforter and I fail to silence my gasps.

"Baby?"

Bash quickly sits up. He scoops his arms beneath me and, as if I were light as a feather, cradles me in his arms. He holds me and rocks but doesn't say a word. He gives me all the time I need to work through my emotions.

I don't know how long he holds me but I feel safe from every cruelty the world has to offer. I gather myself enough to sit up. He brushes the hair off my shoulder as I wipe my tear-soaked cheeks.

I whisper, "I'm sorry. I don't know why…" My words fall away.

He whispers, "Goldie, it's okay."

He doesn't ask me why I cried. He seems to know, even though I don't. He lifts me onto the bathroom counter and wets a washcloth with cool water and wrings it out. As he cleans my face, he seems to understand me better than I understand myself. I watch his eyes and see the depth of his love for me. And that's enough to make me want to cry again.

He sets the cloth in the sink. While his eyes gaze into mine his hands caress down my arms. He takes my hands in his and lifts them to his lips, one at a time, to kiss each tenderly.

"Why did I cry?" I whisper.

"Because you let me in."

CHAPTER FIFTEEN

My alarm screams and I jolt. My dream has left me feeling safe and loved but I can't recall what it was about. I slap the alarm and sit up with a groan. Bash isn't in the bed; he's likely at work already.

There's no coffee made so I start half a pot and stand like a mindless statue as I watch the stream slowly pour. The delicious aroma wakes my mind. I recall how Bash took charge of my body. Damn, that was so hot!

I fill my mug and sip it twice before I do anything. Must. Have. Caffeine. After a quick shower, I dry my hair and apply a little make-up—mostly to draw attention away from the purple bags beneath my eyes.

I hear the front door open and wonder if Bash forgot something.

"Bash?"

Patch's deep voice replies from the bedroom doorway and approaches. "Not Bash. I hope you aren't disappointed." He leans against the doorframe. The way he looks down at me is meant to intimidate me. "Looks like I arrived at the right time."

I'm naked because…

Well, why not? I'm in my bathroom and I was alone. "I wasn't expecting *you* but it's not a bad surprise." I wink. "Aren't you supposed to be tending to Mack?"

"He's a big boy." His eyes take in my nudity. "He fell asleep on the sofa watching television, so I left." He licks his lips. "And I have no regrets."

"Easy, cowboy," I say as I swipe the mascara bristles along my lashes.

"You're putting on make-up." He sighs. "That means you're getting ready for work and probably short on time."

I look over my mascara brush to meet his eyes. "I'm shocked my nudity hasn't clouded your rational thought."

He stands behind me. He isn't coy about where his eyes go. "Oh, don't you worry your pretty little head." His hand glides down my ass cheek and gives it a squeeze. "Nothing's clouding my thinking and my rationality has always been questionable at best." He leans in closer to my shoulder. "Seems you've been marked."

"What? Marked?" I turn to look at my back in the mirror and see a large bite mark. It's tender when I touch it. Under my breath, I whisper, "Now I know what that pain was."

"Bash bit you."

I twist my mouth, unsure if I'm okay with the bite mark or disturbed by it. I open the cabinet and hand a tube of antibiotic cream to Patch. He opens it and puts a glob on his finger. He hands me the tube. With great care, he applies the cream.

He explains, "Maybe he marked you so others will know you're his." Our gaze meets through the mirror and we're both expressionless.

I laugh. "Do you think that's why he bit me; to stake his claim on me?"

His arms wrap around my shoulders until his right-hand cups the left breast and vice versa. He fondles me and I don't stop him. "It doesn't scare me off. If I bite the other shoulder does that mean I own you, too? Maybe Mack should bite you as well. Since both shoulders will have been claimed, I wonder where he'd choose to leave his mark?"

"He'd bite my ass. I'm sure of it." I point through the mirror at him. "You're not biting me so get that out of your head!" I purse my lips and glare at him.

He laughs and shows his teeth as a vampire would. "I'll bite you if I want to." He winks.

"Red."

His smile drops and he frowns. "Fine! No biting." He releases my breasts and slaps my right ass cheek. "I could spank the hell out of you instead."

My pussy twitches. "You could, but I have to go to work."

I brush my hair and pull it into a ponytail. Before I can turn around, Patch has my thighs pressed to the counter with his. He cocks his head and stares at me through the mirror.

"What?" I shake my head and shrug. "Why are you staring at me like that?"

Patch lifts his hands over my shoulders and dangles something in front of me. It's a thin gold necklace. A sparkling white diamond sits in the middle of the star-shaped pendant and catches the light as it swings. He wraps it around my neck and fastens the clasp.

I brush my fingers over it, then lift it to feel its weight. I find his gaze through the mirror. He doesn't wear his familiar rough around the edges expression. Instead, he looks softer somehow.

"Patch, it's beautiful. But why?"

"Because you said having your own star would be awesome and I told you I'd work on it." He kisses the top of my head. "And so you never forget that I love you."

I spin and wrap my arms around his chest. He hugs my head to his chest while his hand rubs my back.

"Thank you. I love it," I whisper and tip my head back to look up at him. "And I love you."

He leans in and kisses me as if it were our first. He's gentle, loving, and yet eager for more. He palms my ass cheeks. Just as he's about to lift me, I break away. I lean against the counter with my arm extended between us.

"As much as I love where this is leading, I have to get ready for work so please stop."

Patch steps back with his hands up in surrender. "Yes, ma'am. I have something to do anyway."

"Good, then leave me be," I say as I shoo him from the bathroom. My fingers graze the pendent once more. I call out,

"And if you drink the rest of the coffee, you'd better make more."

As my shirt slips over my head, Patch grunts in the living room. I pick up my empty mug and rush to see what he's up to. It'd be awesome if he's fucking Lizzy in the kitchen again. It's not likely but a girl can wish, can't she?

The picture Patch hung beside the bay window is now lying on the island. Patch holds a large wooden clock made from the cut slab taken from a wide tree. It's shiny, polished, and beautiful. I set my cup on the island beside the painting and cross the room to get a better look.

He notices me and groans. "You weren't supposed to see it until it was hung."

"Oh, my God! It's so … so … wow!" I say excitedly. He struggles while it slides up and down the wall seeking an anchor. "Can I help?"

"Yeah," he says sharply. "Look behind and find the hook in the wall."

"When did you put that there? It's definitely stronger than the nail was." I hook my finger over it to test its strength and momentarily forget the direness of the situation.

"You were at work." He shifts the heavy clock in his arms. "See the hole in the back of the clock?" I nod. He pants. "Help me line it up."

"Higher," I instruct.

The clock slips onto the hook with ease, much to Patch's relief. I can see the indented red marks from where its weight sat on his arm. He spins the hands to the correct time while I admire his craftsmanship.

He turns and I leap at him. My arms wrap around his neck, my legs around his waist, and I hold on. He grips my ass and his kiss meets my lips with vigor. He's rough with passion and a heady desire. He carries me to the dining room table and sits my ass down. His hand glides up my shirt and cups my breast over my bra.

"How much time do you have?" he asks as he pecks kisses on my neck.

I reply with a breathy whisper. "Less than fifteen minutes."

He jests, "Plenty of time and we can cuddle after."

He yanks me off the table and onto my feet. His fingers find my waistband and tug but the little bow holds them in place.

"No, I don't have time for that," I say, then wave my eyebrows. "Come outside."

Patch wiggles and shifts his semi-erect cock to better position it before he follows me out of the door. I walk to the porch railing and turn around. His questioning leer has me giggling.

"Come here." I glance at my watch. He gets to arm's length and I stop him, unzip his pants and flip the button. The corner of his lip lifts. "You look too happy and that's not doing it for me. Where's the angry man I love to hate?"

"Maybe love to fuck but not hate." He clears his throat and suddenly looks like the familiar, confident man with a dangerous determination to get what he wants. He grips my ponytail and pulls my head back so he can lick my neck and kiss me hard. His fat, strong tongue delves into my mouth to dance with mine.

Our kiss stops and I take in a breath. His face hovers above mine. He whispers with confidence. "You're going to suck my cock." I bite my lip and slink to my knees. He demands, "Take it out."

I slip my hand in his pants and shift his hard cock until it pops free of his black boxer briefs. He's rock-hard. I ask, "May I suck it?"

"I already told you to suck it, don't make me repeat myself."

I wink. "I just wanted to hear you say it again."

He hides his entertainment behind his bad boy expression and watches me take the mushroom head between my lips and roll my tongue over the slit. His nostrils flare and his blink is a few seconds longer.

"Take all of it," he demands.

I take his entire cock down my throat and he rewards me with a moan. I slowly glide my lips to the tip and look up to see him looking out at the forest and not me. When I pause, he glances down. I smile to let him know I want him to watch me pleasure him.

With a crooked smile, his fingers weave into my hair. He pulls and pushes my head how he wants me to suck his cock. He's good not to choke me but sometimes he holds himself down my throat a few seconds too long and I gag. He pulls me back, lets me recover, and does it again. He repeats this eight times.

"You're a very good cock-sucker." He forces me to take him faster into my mouth but doesn't push down my throat. I grab his thighs for assurance. "Put your hands behind your back."

I do what he says and weave my fingers together at my lower back. A sense of helplessness has my heart pounding. I can make it stop if I choose but I pretend I can't and it enhances my fear level.

"That's right. Just like that." He moans. "Be a good whore and make your Master cum."

I hold my throat open and he fucks my mouth deeper.

Surely my mascara has smeared down my cheeks and saliva drips off my chin. I wipe it and hope I won't get any on my uniform.

He breathes erratically and his moan is sharp; he's going to cum. I take a breath and slide him all the way down my throat until my nose presses to his tummy. He cries out as hot jizz shoots down my throat. I gag but try to relax my throat. Slowly, I let his cock ease from my throat but his seed still spits onto my tongue. I suck hard and he grabs my head. I suck and release repeatedly until his body jerks, followed by a lengthy exhale.

Patch looks at me with a flushed face and a gaping mouth. He takes my hand and helps me to my feet. His thumbs wipe my cheeks to rid the spilled tears but his grimace tells me I need to fix my make-up.

He kisses me tenderly. "Too rough?"

I shake my head. "A bit but I liked the control you had over me, Master."

"I could get used to you calling me Master and sucking my cock outside."

I wink and slip from his clutches. "Think of it as payment for my star necklace and the fucking amazing clock. They're both beautiful, by the way."

"You once said you loved the clock we have at the main house so I wanted to build one for you, too."

"You're so damn talented!" I kiss him once more, then disappear into the house. His truck drives away before I've made it to the bathroom.

CHAPTER SIXTEEN

The patients seem to come and go through the operating room as if on a conveyor belt. The surgeries today are quick and repetitive, which means nothing of interest like a knife to the chest, for instance. Not that I'd want anyone to go through that, but it would make for an interesting day.

Today, eighty-seven-year-old Mr. Lennysman will have a lump removed from his throat. Surgery at his age holds higher risks but it's beginning to impede his trachea so it's necessary. I check him in while he chats with me about how nosy the townsfolk are and how they should stay out of my love life. He told me that some time ago when the shit first hit the fan, so to speak. He told me to enjoy my life and do what makes me happy. He's a sweet man and I hope he recovers from this.

An hour passes quickly as I tend to more patients. Lizzy, who's been assisting in surgery today, strolls up to the desk with a sucker wedged between her puffy, pink lips.

"Hey, sexy baby!" she jests with a swing of her hips. "Mr. Lennysman is out of surgery. Before we put him under, he asked me to relay a message." She tilts her head. "He said, 'They can either accept you or they can fuck off.' Then he apologized for the vulgar language. I'm not even going to ask what the hell that's all about but I'm sure it's an interesting story."

I chuckle. "Private joke. How did his surgery go?" I ask while I tidy the desk.

She shrugs and scrunches her face. "It looks like cancer."

"Oh, shit!" I sag. "I'll have to stop in to see him before I go home." I groan and lean back in the chair and rest my forearms over my eyes.

She slides her ass onto the desk and pulls the sucker from her mouth with a pop. "Okay, fill me in. What's up with you today?"

I sigh, drop my arms, and spin my chair left to right to rock myself. "I'm sexually frustrated thanks to Patch."

"Patch left you sexually frustrated? That doesn't sound like him." She wiggles on the desk until she's further back so she can use the faded pink wall as a backrest.

I giggle and roll my chair forward and rest my elbows on the desk and my chin on my fists. "Patch came over this morning. Bash had already left for work. Patch gave me this necklace." She leans in to get a closer look and then frowns as if to ask why. "Something he said about giving me everything, even a star if I asked for it."

"Ah," she says with a tilted head. "That's so sweet." She tastes the lollipop, then pulls it from her lips. "Patch. Hot, sexy Patch left you sexually frustrated."

"I wasn't in the mood for a quick fuck." I half-shrug. "So I sucked his cock on the porch."

Her eyelids droop and she licks her lips. "So, you have a belly full of cum and a dripping wet pussy that aches for cock. You poor thing!"

"Oh!" I sit straight up. "I completely forgot! Mack had an accident last night."

Her face scrunches and she swats my arm. "Why wouldn't you lead with that?"

I feign severe pain. "He's okay but he broke his arm and fractured his clavicle, a gash, bruised ribs. Patch's playing nurse to make sure he takes his pills. We have yet to compare schedules so he isn't left alone for any length of time, at least for the next few days."

"Well, if you can use me, call me."

I shake my head. "I can't ask you to do that."

She scowls. "You aren't asking, I'm offering." She glances at her watch and slides off the desk. "Besides, I want to meet the pretty-boy with the long hair and seductive blue eyes." She waves her eyebrows.

"He's a beautiful man," I moan. "And he loves anal."

She looks around but the hall is empty. She grabs her ass and humps backward. She whispers, "Fuck my ass! Give it to me, pretty boy!"

I burst into laughter but slap my hand over my mouth to regain some control. She laughs and waves as she retreats down the hallway and reminds me to call her just as she rounds the corner.

After my shift ends, I stop in to see Mr. Lennysman. They'd moved him from recovery to intensive care. The nurse said he's not doing well. He still hasn't awakened and isn't responding to stimuli. I know he might not survive through the night.

I hold his hand and whisper in his ear. "Mr. Lennysman, I got your message and I agree; they can either accept us or fuck off." I snicker. "Thank you for being kind to me. I wish you happiness and peace."

CHAPTER SEVENTEEN

Bash isn't home when I arrive. He called to say he'll be working late at the *Daily News*. Ever since they promoted him to an editor's position, his workdays are getting longer and longer and he doesn't have as much freedom to work from home.

Patch is working at the mill until late tonight. Shaina said she'd stay the night to care for Mack. I sent her a text but she hasn't gotten back to me. I had doubts she would but I need to know if I'm still supposed to bring dinner over, which were the arrangements.

I take the chicken breasts from the fridge and prepare them so they'll have a spicy, crunchy coating, then space them out on a baking sheet. After I peel potatoes, I check my phone. Still no reply from her. After the chicken and cheesy potatoes are in the oven, I wash the dishes then take a quick shower and slip into yoga pants, a white t-shirt, and a long button-up sweater that I leave unbuttoned. I put everything in my car and drive to the main house.

I carry the potatoes first and knock on the door but quickly push it open. They're so hot! I rush to the stove and put it down. I turn and rush back out the door to get the chicken. Shaina comes out of the bathroom just as I close the door.

She stands with her hands on her waist, hip jutted out and glowering. "What are you doing here?" she whispers condescendingly.

"I brought dinner," I reply and refrain from including the sarcastic comments that whirl around in my thoughts. "We agreed to it last night."

"*We*," she says with great emphasis, "did not. I can cook for my man."

"And you can afford to buy his lunch. I get it. This isn't a pissing contest. Bash had to stay late at work. Patch is at the mill until later and since it was already arranged that I would cook dinner and nobody called to change the plans, I assumed I still would be. You obviously didn't get my text, otherwise, you could have let me know you'd be here to feed and tend to him."

We stand in silence for several seconds while she scans me top to bottom. Her lip quirks. "I already ordered a pizza. It should be here in about half an hour. But thanks anyway."

"I'm going to check in on him," I say, not giving her a chance to deny me.

"He's asleep," she says as I pass by her.

I peek into his room, and it's dark and I can hear his light snores. Damn, he is asleep. I was going to ask him what he prefers to eat for dinner. If he chose pizza, I'd be okay with that, as long as it's his choice.

I make my way back to the kitchen island where she set the food to wait for me to take home. I ask, "Did you order enough for Patch or should I wrap some chicken up for him?"

"Oh, I plan to stay all night so Patch can stay here with me or go be with you. I don't care either way."

Laughter escapes me. "That's not what I asked. Patch often comes here to eat and then comes home to us. I just need to know if I should leave food for him or not."

"I ordered a king-sized pizza, fully loaded. There will be plenty," she insists.

I pick up the food and walk to the door. She opens it for me. As I step out, I pause to look at her with a pitiful expression because I know it'll piss her off. "You have problems, lady."

"Oh, *I* have problems?" She hisses as she follows me out to my car.

Over my shoulder, I reply, "Obviously! When you first started dating Mack, he told you he fucks around with other women. You said you were okay with it but now you aren't? Or is it just me you don't like?"

As I set the food on the roof and open my car door then put the food on the passenger's seat, she yells, "You weren't satisfied with the man you already have, so you take another man's heart. And the greedy bitch you are, you want my man's heart, too. Even after I asked you to back off, you still come around and want to play nursemaid."

I really want to punch her lights out! Instead, I lean on the driver's seat and set the food on the floor in case something leaks. "He's broken! Forgive me for checking in on him. I AM A NURSE!"

She points her finger at me as she nears me. "He doesn't need you for anything. He has me. I … will take care … of *my* man. No more hugs, no more loving kisses, and don't even think about fucking him."

"Didn't we already go through this in the restaurant? You want me to leave Mack alone? Fine! When he tells me to stay away from him, I will, but—"

She hisses, "I don't need you spreading your bad boojoo all over my man, too. You've already got Patch and Bash twirling around your little finger, dancing like puppets at your beck and call. Do you really want to turn the third brother into a sucker, too?"

"SHAINA!" Mack shouts from ten feet behind her. We both startle. She spins and I bump my head on the doorframe. "What the hell is wrong with you?"

"I'm just suggesting she—"

He doesn't let her finish. "You should go now."

Stunned, she takes a step back. Calmly, she asks, "What? You want *me* to leave?"

Mack slowly nods. "Yes, I think you should." He walks toward her. "When we started dating, I explained in detail that Goldilocks will be in my life and my bed forever, and you will need to accept that or walk away. You chose to accept my lifestyle and this is how I catch you speaking to her."

With wide eyes, she walks to him and starts to explain. "I only meant that she—"

"No woman of mine will insult or threaten Goldilocks. She belongs here." With little expression, he dismisses her. "You can go."

She storms into the house; the screen door slams behind her and I can hear her stomps in the house. A few seconds later, she rushes out while she mumbles to herself. She spits a few choice words loud enough for us to hear and throws her purse in her car.

Before she gets in she yells at Mack. "What are you going to do when she chooses Bash, leaving you and Patch to pine over that little twat? Huh? I know, you're going to become hard and numb like Patch already is. Enjoy your misery! And, *Goldilocks*," she says my name with the sarcasm of a teenager. "Fuck you, cunt!"

I yell back, "I've been called worse by Patch. You've only succeeded in turning me on."

She screeches at me and shoots me the middle finger. Her car whips down the driveway and around the bend so quickly Mack and I wince and wait to hear the crunch of her fender against a tree. Surprisingly, she doesn't hit it.

"I'm sorry, Goldilocks. I didn't know she was like that." He wraps an arm around my shoulders. "Why didn't you tell me she confronted you at the diner? And when did this happen?"

I lift my face and kiss him just once. "You were paying. Mack, I'm a big girl and can handle my own battles. I thought she'd calm down at some point."

"It's not only your battle though, Goldilocks. It's mine too; I brought her into our lives. It's only right that you should have talked to me when she became a problem." He brushes a lock of my blonde hair behind my ear. "I'm starving."

"Oh, I made chicken and cheesy potatoes but Shaina said—"

He shakes his head. "I don't care what she said, I care about my growling stomach." He leans to smell the food and sighs his approval.

Just as I pick up the container and the toweled glass dish, a car rounds the bend and stops beside us. A teenager climbs out, opens the back door, and takes a king-sized pizza from the warming bag.

He says, "Whoever just left here nearly hit me."

"Oh, sorry about that." I apologize on her behalf and then look at Mack who doesn't know why the kid is here. "Shaina ordered pizza. She didn't know I was cooking."

"She knew! I heard Patch tell her." He looks at the kid who holds the large box. "Can I refuse that pizza and have it sent elsewhere? I'll give you a tip for your trouble but I'm not paying for a pizza I didn't ask for."

The scruffy kid looks confused. "It's already paid for." He looks at the name written on the receipt. "Someone named Shaina paid for it with a credit card." He shrugs. "Do you still want me to take it somewhere else?"

"Well, since it's already paid for!" I set the food on the hood of my car and then take the pizza from the kid. My smile isn't for the free pizza. I wear it because accepting it is a little *fuck you* to Shaina.

Mack snickers and gives the kid a tip. He thanks him and hops back in the tiny car and speeds away; not nearly as fast as Shaina.

We eat both my dinner and some of the pizza while we discuss topics that range from our high school days, past relationships, and even touch on politics. Mack's eyelids weigh heavily. Despite his denial, I know he's tired so I insist he gets into bed.

"Lie with me?" he asks as I pull the comforter up to his chin and tuck it around the cast as best I can.

I reply, "If I do, I'll end up falling asleep and Bash won't appreciate me spending the night with you; it's one of the rules. Do you have everything you need?"

His eyebrows raise, then he lifts the sheet and looks down. "I have a … small problem."

I look under the sheet and see that his erection tents his pale blue pajama bottoms.

"That does look like a problem, but it's not small."

I flop the blankets back and pull down on the waistband until his hard prick pops free. It stands at attention before me. I wrap my lips around the head and glide as far down as I can. He moans appreciatively.

His cock is longer but thinner than both Bash and Patch which is perfect for anal sex, which is his kink. He took my anal cherry so to speak.

I bob on his prick and suck and swirl the head.

"Take your clothes off and sit on my face." He moans. "Let me taste your pussy. Please?" he begs between pants.

I shake my head and continue my delicious assault. I cup and squeeze his balls just right. I grip the base of his cock in my other hand. He moans out and his hips lift.

"Oh, fuck! Goldilocks…" He wails while his body jerks and he fills my mouth with his seed. I swallow and continue to glide up and down as he twitches and whimpers. "I fucking love your mouth! I love you!"

I wipe my mouth as I tuck him back in. His eyelids hang and his blinks are progressively becoming longer. I kiss his forehead and whisper, "I love you, too, and I'm sorry about Shaina." He shakes his head so I grow a half-smile. "Go to sleep."

His smile fades as his eyelids close.

After I text Patch to see when I should expect his arrival, he immediately writes back and says he'll be here shortly. I let him know I'm going home and there's food in the fridge. He begs me to stay so he can repay me for this morning but I kindly decline.

I lock up and drive home. Bash is eating the food I left in the fridge for him in the living room while he watches television.

As I set my purse on the bench by the door, I snicker. "I'd come to kiss you but I need to brush my teeth first."

A potato wedge hangs off his fork and he gives me a sideways glance. "Patch?" He shoves the fork in his mouth.

"I blew Patch this morning," I confess with a shrug. "But Mack felt a little lonely so I blew him, too." Bash snickers. I progress toward him with my arms crossed over my chest. "I think him and Shaina are finished."

He looks surprised. "That's too bad. Do you know what happened?"

Mack overheard her yelling at me. She's been a bitch to me lately. I thought she'd work past it but…" I shrug.

His forehead crinkles. "How come you didn't tell me?"

I shrug to blow it off. "Like I said, I figured we'd work it out."

"Mhm." He doesn't look satisfied with my answer. "If you have a problem with someone we bring into our circle, you have to speak up. Promise me."

After a long sigh, I reply, "Deal."

He tilts his head and raises his eyebrows. "So you sucked two cocks today, huh?" He lifts his plate and I can see the bulge tucked away in his jeans. "Want to try for three?"

"Can I brush my teeth first?" I tease. "Unless you want me to kiss you with Mack's cum in my teeth."

He grimaces. "You don't have to kiss me if you're just going to blow me, but … EWW!" He stabs a piece of chicken. "Mouthwash twice, okay?"

I laugh as I walk through the kitchen and down the hall to the master bathroom. After a shower and hearty mouth cleansing—as requested—I slip on matching red stockings, garter belt, bra, and black high-heels, and then send him a text to ask if he can help me with a box in the bedroom.

He enters and his eyes light up. He immediately strips off his clothes with lightning speed. He bites his lip as he struts toward me; his huge, steel-hard cock swings as he does. He grips it and slowly strokes as his eyes drink me in. "So, you have a box that you need help with?" Before he scoops me up and tosses me onto the bed, he whispers, "Girl, you are in for it tonight."

He's on me quickly and kisses me while his hands grope my body. Bash moans and slips down. He jiggles my bra cup until my nipple pops free below the underwire. He sucks and laps on it while he frees the other. He nips and sucks my nipples and my pussy clenches, eager to feel the heat of his mouth. Slowly, he kisses down my tummy while his beautiful blue eyes burn into mine.

His hands glide along my thighs then spread them wide. He kisses my panties before he gently pulls them aside. With a flat tongue, he licks from asshole to clit and sucks my swelling button before he laps at it with a fury. I grip the light grey comforter and hang on as I fall deeper and deeper into my body; into the mind-numbing deliciousness of orgasm.

No thoughts. No control. Stupendous pleasure.

I revel in the aftermath of so much pleasure. He tenderly pecks kisses on my twitching clit while it sends shockwaves through my entire body. It's both wonderful and painful.

Bash rushes up my body and fills me with his thick, hard cock. My nails dig into his waist to pull him in. My cries are met with his lips. His hips pound against me. My legs, as if having a mind of their own, wrap around his waist so my pussy can pull him in further, so the tip of his cock can torture my cervix.

He lifts himself up and grabs my panties and yanks them down my legs and tosses them aimlessly. He's inside me again and pounding himself deep into me as he watches the action.

He groans, "Fuck, you're so beautiful."

Before I can react, he's up on his knees. He has my right leg on the bed between his legs, and my left leg bent at the knee and pressed against my chest. He turns me so my left leg crosses my body and then slams deeper into me than I've ever had anyone. At first, I'm shocked by the pain of the depth but my body surprises me and spins me into a screaming orgasm, and then another, and another.

I have no idea how much time passes or how many orgasms I've screamed through, but I've found my new favorite position. Bash pulls out of me, grips his cock, and begins to jerk himself off.

"No, please," I beg. "I want you in my mouth."

He grips the leg lying straight on the bed and my shoulder and spins me so I'm on my tummy facing him. I lift myself on my arms and open my mouth. He holds my head and fucks my mouth but refrains from pushing into my throat. I push myself onto him to take more.

"Shit! I'm going to cum, baby," he mutters, then his tummy muscles lock tight to reveal washboard abs.

I pull my legs beneath me and grip the base of his cock tightly while I suck and bob. His wail cuts short as his body seizes and jerks. Seed fills my mouth for the third time today. I wonder if people would refer to me as a cum-guzzling whore if they ever found out. I don't care, my men are satisfied and they don't disrespect me for my whorish behavior.

Bash falls to the bed and pulls me with him. I land with my head on his shoulder. Slowly our gasps ease and the brightly lit room is quiet.

"Goddamn, Goldie," he pauses. "You drive me fucking nuts because you're perfect in every way."

"I'm not perfect; I have flaws," I retort.

"I don't care about your damn flaws." He turns his head to look into my eyes. He kisses me with velvety softness. "My love for you is infinite. And my brothers love you, too. One day, you'll really be ours."

My eyebrows lift. "What does that mean?"

"It means I'm going to marry you one day."

I smile, kiss him quickly, then slide out of bed. "Yeah, we'll see," I tease as my wobbly legs carry me to the bathroom.

He calls after me. "Yeah, we'll see! You'll see." In a whisper so quiet I'm sure it wasn't meant for me to hear, he says, "Sooner than later."

CHAPTER EIGHTEEN

Getting to work with ten minutes to spare is a windfall for me; I usually run in at the last minute. I go to check on Mr. Lennysman but I'm told he passed away during the night, having never woke from surgery.

Maybe I should have stayed and talked to him to give him some comfort. He died alone in a cold, bright, sterile room. Surely he deserved better than that.

Between my first and second surgery, I text Bash to let him know about Mr. Lennysman. He writes back immediately that he's sad to hear and how he really liked the old dude; his words, not mine.

Lizzy is nothing if not a woman who isn't afraid to do silly shit simply to lift my spirits. She's quickly become one of my favorite people.

For the first surgery, she drew a goofy smile on her surgical mask but it was missing a few teeth. The fourth surgery had her smoking a cigar. The sixth, she was puckering up for a kiss. It kept me entertained but Dr. Kacey didn't seem all too amused. He sensed I was upset about something and was kind-hearted enough not to ask her to cut it out.

"Lizzy?"

She replies, "Yes, dear Goldilocks."

"Are you busy tonight? Any grand plans?"

She replies in a high pitch, Alabama accent, "No, ma'am. I am free as a jaybird. Why? Do you want to get drunk tonight and have your way with me?"

Dr. Kacey looks at her and clears his throat and then glances at me.

I stutter, "She's kidding. We, we don't … do that." His eyes drop to my chest and to the patient to continue the surgery.

Her eyebrows dance and she giggles. "Do you want to do something tonight?"

I can smell the stench from the cauterization. "Actually, I thought I could introduce you to Mack."

Just by her tone, I can tell she's smiling. "I'm finally going to meet that stud-muffin? I. Am. In!"

"Okay, pick me up at my place at six and we can go together."

She enthusiastically asks, "Where's Patch going to be?"

I giggle. "He'll be at the mill, and I don't know what time he'll be done."

She pouts. "Damn, I was hoping to *see* him again."

***

Lizzy parks her burgundy Jeep beside my car. She's wearing snug black jeans and a white V-neck cashmere sweater. Her hair is wavy with perfect curls and her make-up looks freshly applied.

I lean on the open-door frame and whistle as she ascends the stairs. "Damn, woman! You're gorgeous!" I whistle again and she does a little twirl and flips her hair.

"Thank you," she says, then looks past me into the house. "Bash home?"

A smile grows on my face. I sing, "You want him. You want him. Hell yeah, you want him."

Her palms lift. "You make it sound like I'm going to hop on his cock before we say hello. Although that sounds like fun, I'd like to meet Mack."

I shut the door and start down the stairs while she follows. "That's too bad. I'm sure he'd love to *say hello* to you, too."

I direct her as she drives to the main house. She follows me inside while she compliments on how quaint and relaxing the setting is. Mack is in the kitchen munching on potato chips. They're scattered on the counter, floor, and table.

"Jeeze, Mack! Did you get any in your mouth?" I tease and start to pick them off the floor.

"I couldn't open the bag so I used my teeth." His toothy smile has his face even more handsome than it already was.

I hear Lizzy whisper under her breath. "Goddamn. Not an ugly brother in the bunch."

"How rude of me," I say and step to the side as Lizzy nears us. Mack licks his lips and doesn't blink. "Mack, this is Lizzy. Lizzy, meet Mack."

Mack whispers, "Patch wasn't bullshitting. You are gorgeous!" He looks at me as if to give me shit for not having introduced them months ago. "I'd shake your hand, but…" He points to his cast held against his bare chest by a dark-blue sling. His loose-fitting black pajama pants flow as he walks to the fridge and it's obvious he's going commando. "Can I get anyone a beer?"

"I'll take one," I say and look at Lizzy who has yet to avert her eyes from Mack's body. "Make it two." He takes three out. "None for you. You're medicated."

Lizzy sees his sexy glare and whimpers but quickly recovers by clearing her throat. "You have a great house, Mack." She slowly walks away as she turns to admire the room.

"Thank you. It keeps the rain off." Mack admires her breasts, but when she walks away, he tilts his head and sways his hips. His gaze meets mine and he silently mouths *great ass!* "Would you like me to show you around?"

I open his bottle of water and hand it to him. He takes a gulp and pouts when I lift my beer and sip it.

She takes a beer and follows him around the house. I stay in the kitchen to sweep up the chip crumbs and then prepare a couple of ham sandwiches for Mack. When they return, it's obvious both are smitten with each other. I refill Mack's water bottle, then we all sit and watch him eat while we chit chat.

An hour later, when Lizzy's in the washroom, Mack tilts his head toward the ceiling. "That fucking chick could be the death of me and I'd welcome it. Fuckin' Patch got to her first." His mouth sets in a hard line.

"I'm sure if you asked nicely, he'd be willing to share the shiny new toy but it's up to her, of course."

"Of course," he repeats and his eyes narrow as he surveys me. "And you, too."

"Me?" My forehead furrows.

He looks down at his bottle. "How would you feel about it if we hooked up?"

"She can do anything she likes because I trust her." I take a long gulp of beer while my eyes remain fixed on his. "She's fucking hot! I would fuck her if I had a cock and if I were into pussy. I just might be willing to hop the fence for a little ménage."

"I'd pay a hefty price to sit in the corner and watch that." He looks vacantly past me as if watching it play out in his mind. He rests his casted arm on the table. "So...?" he questions with round eyes.

I laugh. "So, go for it! I'm sure Patch wouldn't mind. I'll text him if it'll make you feel better."

He says, "It would."

I pick up my phone while Mack hums a happy tune with a smile plastered on his face. I set my phone down and laugh at his silly display of excitement.

He asks, "What about you and Bash? Have you two considered taking her to bed?"

"I've been thinking a lot about it and I want to see Bash and her in a sweaty heap; moaning, licking, and fucking each other. Just thinking about it revs me up. But I'm not sure I have the courage to get in on something like that just yet."

"Goldie-girl," she says as she crosses the room toward the table and does a little hop before she sits. My phone chimes when she says, "We should give Patch a night off from babysitting Mack. Why don't I," her gaze falls to Mack "stay here with Mack, so Patch can spend the night with you and Bash?" Faking innocence, she adds, "I can sleep on the couch."

Mack looks at me to judge my reaction to the text message. I meet his gaze and the corners of my lips lift. We simultaneously agree that she should stay. I think we're all going to win tonight! Half-hour later, I take a flashlight and head off into the woods and leave the two of them to whatever mischief they can get into.

I'm immersed in the darkness of the night. The shadows cast from the roots of the fallen trees resemble bears or wolves ready to attack. It's hard to keep myself calm even though I've grown up in these woods and have yet to hear of a bear or wolf attack on a human. Lizzy offered to drive me home but I refused it. I love the forest; day or night.

When I arrive home, Bash tells me Patch just got in the shower in his ensuite bathroom.

With wide eyes, I say, "I haven't showered in there yet. Have you?"

"Nope." Bash tilts his head away from the television as he tosses a peanut in his mouth. "Well, I think it's about time you do. Don't you?"

"We aren't going to fuck," I say and he gives me a confused look. "I don't want to tire him out. I plan to take you both to bed tonight if that's okay with you."

"Patch said he was going to the main house tonight to help Mack."

I wave my eyebrows. "No need. Lizzy's there and I think they're going to get along swimmingly."

"Oh!" he says with a naughty grin. "That means you get both of us tonight. I hope you had a nap today; you're going to need it."

My pussy clenches at the image of me sandwiched between them while they kiss me everywhere and drown me in euphoria. "I'm going to go join Patch and then I'm going to get into bed to wait for my two studs."

"I'll be there," he promises. I kiss him, then rush to join Patch.

Patch washes every inch of my skin, then my hair. I do absolutely nothing to help, as per his wishes. He takes extra care to ensure my vagina and nipples are well washed, he even drops to his knees to taste me just to make sure I'm clean. He dries me and wraps me in a fluffy yellow towel. He dries himself then takes my hand to lead me through the house to the master bathroom where Bash showers. He has me sit on the stool while he blow-dries my hair and Bash rinses off.

The two stand behind me with towels around their waists. My eyes shift between their well-formed arms, chests, abs, and bulges. My legs squeeze together to stifle my pussy's hunger.

Bash watches Patch work the hairdryer as best he can for a man whose hair has always been cropped army short. As he puts away the dryer, Bash brushes out the knots.

"Would you like me to put it in a ponytail?" I look from man to man.

Patch's mouth twists as he considers. Bash asks, "Can you braid it?"

They have identical deep creases on their foreheads as they watch my hands flip tresses of hair this way and that.

I stand and turn to face them. I am a lucky woman!

CHAPTER NINETEEN

Bash takes my hand. I stand and follow him as he walks backward toward the bed. He stops a few feet from it. Patch slides my towel from my body. He stands so close behind me I can feel his heat. His lips press feathery soft to the back of my neck and I shudder. Bash kisses my lips just as tenderly. My knees weaken.

Patch whispers just behind my left ear. "We're going to bind you in rope. You won't be able to use your hands or arms. We will do everything for you." He kisses me again. "Do you trust us to keep you safe?"

"Yes." My whisper is barely audible.

Bash sits on the bed. A brown rope with a scent I'm not familiar with is held in front of me by Patch. I watch him undo the tan-colored rope and run his hands along it as if he treasures it.

He moans softly. "There's nothing sexier than a woman bound in rope, giving herself to me and entrusting me to protect her."

Patch loops the rope over my neck and begins tying the two ropes together with small knots about four inches apart. Each line of rope runs between my legs, up my back, and through the loop at the back of my neck. The ropes are separated and fed under my armpits and then looped through one of the four-inch sections before it returns under my arms to loop around the rope lining my spine.

He repeats once more but has me hold one rope end in my mouth while he wraps my left arm three times, then knots it somehow. He relieves me of the rope and repeats with my right arm. He continues to wrap my torso but stops twice more to incorporate my arms in the binds. As he continues, the two ropes that run through my pussy pull tighter and tighter.

When I wiggle, Patch has concerns. "Are you in pain?"

I shake my head. "It's pressing on my pussy."

Bash asks, "Do you like the way it feels?"

I wiggle again. "Yes, but the placement is off."

He sinks to his knees and guides the ropes until they each lie in the leg's crease on either side of my pussy. Now they squeeze my labia together. I moan and Bash's lip lifts at the corner as his eyes burn into mine.

Bash sits back on the bed to watch Patch enjoy his rope-play as if to bind me is his most intimate way for us to connect. He stands before me to tie the final knot. His face isn't rough and angry as is his usual expression; he seems softer somehow as though his mind has quieted. He could say he loves me a hundred times but at this moment, the way his fingers trace the ropes that line my skin, he's not just watching me; his soul watches mine. The peaceful silence screams love.

He slips a finger under the knot between my breasts and leads me. Their towels fall to the floor as they crawl onto the bed. Bash lies on his back and Patch maneuvers me so I kneel on either side of Bash's head, my pussy hovers above his lips. Bash's hands pull down on my hips until my labia presses to his mouth. The restriction from the ropes and the way his tongue fishes between my lips has me edged so close to orgasm in an instant. Perhaps ropes are my kink, too.

Patch instructs me. "Don't cum."

This will not be easy. I wince when he pinches my nipples with wooden clothespins. He kisses me tenderly, then his tongue glides along my upper lip.

He whispers, "You are so fucking beautiful."

Patch stands on either side of Bash's waist and grips my braid to guide my mouth around his rock-hard cock. I lick and suck him while Bash does the same to me. It feels so good that I get lost in it and forget about Patch.

He steps aside and grasps the rope on my back. He slowly lowers me until my mouth lines up with Bash's cock. Patch releases the ropes.

I do my best to mouth the huge cock but without the ability to raise my chest, it's a rather pathetic attempt at oral copulation. Bash lifts me by my ribs and rests his elbows on the bed at his waist. It's a little easier this way.

I fight the urge to orgasm by lifting my pussy off his face for a few seconds until the tension eases. Patch steps up on the bed and slips his fingers under the crisscrossed ropes by my shoulder blades and down at my lower back. He lifts me using the ropes. I hover, suspended over Bash, who slides up the bed and stops.

Patch lowers me and Bash spreads my knees, then uses my hips to guide my pussy over his cock. Patch lowers me slowly and releases me only when I've enveloped every inch of Bash's erection. With the aid of the ropes, Bash guides my movements so I rock on his cock how he wants me to move.

This is so fucking sexy, but I wish I wasn't backward because I want to watch Bash's face as I ride him. Does he love the ropes as much as I do?

Patch stands over Bash's legs and again grips my braid to aim my mouth so I can suck him. He's more forceful this time and holds himself in my throat a few seconds longer than I desire but I trust in him not to hurt me.

An orgasm rolls through me. I couldn't hold it off any longer, and I couldn't ask permission because of the cock in my throat. Bash holds himself inside me. His moans prove he favors my vaginal spasms as my orgasm slowly concludes.

Patch feeds his fingers beneath the ropes at my shoulder blades and tailbone and lifts. I'm suspended again, aside from my feet that hope to find their footing on the bed. He steps off the bed and I swing and scream, then laugh. It looks like I'm going to hit the floor face first but he has me safely in his clutches.

I laugh again but I don't know why. Is it because I didn't die just now or because I love the thrill of it all?

A waist-high A-frame bench with a leather padded top has me curious where it came from. I would have noticed it there when I came into the room. Patch sets me so that I lie over it, face down. My chest hangs over one end and my legs the other. I look under the bench and see Patch squatted behind me.

Using three leather straps on each leg, he binds my legs securely to the A-frame. Two more straps wrap over my torso and arms like seatbelts and fasten tightly. I can barely move.

I'm scared and yet more aroused than I've ever been. What will they do to me? Will I like it? My chest has limited movement but the rest of me is locked down and at their mercy.

"What's your safeword, Goldie?" Bash stands a few inches in front of my face while he strokes his heavy cock. Patch's hands slap down on my ass and I jolt.

"Red," I reply while I twist my upper body and neck, attempting to look at his face. I smile when I understand my limitations and then relax back into position.

Patch fiddles with my braid but Bash's hand gliding up and down his cock holds my interest. The ropes that lead between my ass cheeks are yanked and then yanked again until they slip over my buttocks and are no longer wedged between the globes. The ropes hold my pussy lips apart and the air feels icy as it teases my superheated flesh.

Patch slides his cock into my pussy and holds himself inside while he fiddles with the knotted rope near my ass. My braid pulls and my head tilts until my mouth is perfectly lined up to take a penis. He ties it, then fucks me; hard and fast.

Bash slips the fat mushroom head between my lips and I suck like there's no tomorrow. I want him in my throat. I want my whole body full of them.

Take me! Take all of me!

He slowly fucks my mouth but not nearly as hard, fast, or deep as Patch takes my pussy. I can't move and the weight of my torso pressing into the bench makes it that much harder to breathe, but I love the restriction. Patch slows and something cold drips on my asshole. His finger slips in while he continues to fuck me but with an easier rhythm.

Bash eases his cock from my lips and bends to kiss me with vigor. His hand wraps around my throat and applies a little pressure on either side of my trachea to slow my blood flow to my brain. I'm lightheaded but I'm not afraid; I like it. Patch stretches my asshole while my pussy clenches his cock and my mind whirls.

The tip of Patch's cock presses into my ass and it welcomes him. Bash's grip eases as his lips and tongue assault my mouth. Patch eases into me and I moan. My throat is set free and Bash stands and then pushes the head of his cock in my mouth. I suck while Patch slowly fucks my ass. His cock is thicker than Mack's, and I can definitely feel the difference but it's wonderful.

The rope that held my braid is removed. My head hangs while Patch slowly glides in and out of my asshole while Bash frees my legs and then my torso. Patch slips out of my ass and lifts me by the ropes. He carries me to the bed like a sack of potatoes with legs and I giggle.

Bash lies on his back on the bed. Patch sets me on my knees on the bed and Bash grips my chest ropes and guides me until I can straddle him. His prick is quickly devoured by my wanton pussy. I immediately slide back and forth greedily. Patch moves in behind me and slips his knees between my calves and Bash's thighs. My knees are spread very wide.

Using the ropes bound over my chest, Bash pulls me down on him but stops me just before our faces collide. He holds me in place and kisses me softly, seductively. Patch gently slips his cock back into my ass and pauses to give my body time to adjust to the overwhelming fullness.

I can't kiss. I can't moan. I can barely breathe. I've never been this full in my entire life. The skin on my back beneath Patch's kisses prickles in the wake of his hot breath.

Beneath me, Bash lifts his hips to press himself deeper into me while Patch gradually retreats, then eases all the way back in again. They mold into me with a slow passion and it's deliriously marvelous.

My hips are lifted an inch or so, and then I'm lowered. Something cold is placed between me and Bash, up against my clit. It suddenly springs to life with mild vibration.

I might be drooling. I can't be sure. "Oh, God! Please…"

As they continue to fuck me, the vibration increases and my body stiffens. The tightness in my tummy is so immense, like an expanded balloon. If I cum it might be too much and I may die but I don't care.

They fuck faster and the vibration revs into warp speed. I jerk and mumble sounds that don't form words. I fall further and further into a black hole, yet somehow I'm afloat near the ceiling. My entire being twitches and the vibrator slips to the exact spot on my clit and I'm drowning in the peacefulness of euphoria.

I'm lost. My soul is gone, or maybe I am only a soul now and I've left my body. I feel nothing except immense pleasure that can't be measured or explained. It just is…

Someone screams and I fall back into my body. It was me; I screamed. Both men use me like an old whore and I can't get enough.

"Yes! Fuck me!" I yell as the sweat between our bodies builds. "Ah, gaaa! Fu…" My thoughts spin wildly until they no longer exist. I don't exist. Nothing does. Absolutely nothing.

A barbaric groan vibrates my back and prickles my skin with its heat. Patch wails again, then quickly pulls himself from my ass and sinks to the end of the bed. His grunt echoes about the room. His breath holds—he's coming, hard!

Bash wraps his arm around me and rolls us both. I'm below him and try to see his features through blurred vision. He lifts my knees and spreads them, then sinks his thick cock into my pussy. He leans forward to rest his weight on his forearms. His lips press to mine and hold. He's not delving his tongue or trying to advance our kiss. He fucks me and he's lost.

He whispers, "I love you. I love you. I love you. I love y—"

Bash's breath holds and his body stills, and then jerks. His cock throbs inside me as he fills me with his seed. His exasperated exhale has his tension slowly easing.

His eyes remain closed and he drops his forehead to my shoulder. He whispers, "I love you so much." He shudders, whimpers, and then swallows hard. His exhale is long and hot on my neck.

My breath slowly calms. I want to hold him, but my arms are still bound by my sides. I settle for resting my cheek against his forehead. His softened penis slips from me and we both groan from the disappointment. He lifts his face to kiss me.

"Let's get her untied," Patch interrupts our moment with as soft a voice as he can manage.

Bash smiles then kisses me before he helps me onto my feet. My knees are weak and my entire existence is spent. If I could see my soul, it would look disheveled and exhausted but smiling and utterly satisfied.

I'm silent as the ropes glide against my skin. Patch's eyes lock on mine when they can, and I miss them when he's behind me. The love I see in his eyes screams volumes. Even the world's best poets couldn't put into words the love these men have shown me tonight.

As the ropes glide and edge me toward freedom, I understand why Patch has a bondage fetish. My trust in him means everything to him and I can feel that through the ropes as they caress my flesh.

The rope lifts from around my neck, and I'm freed. Patch looks at my face as if to memorize my features. "Goldilocks, you own my heart. I will always be here for you. Even when I'm not, I'm still here." He lifts my hand and sets my palm over his heart. "It beats for you."

Bash stands next to Patch. He lifts my other hand, tips his head toward me, and sets my hand on it. "You already know you own me … you own all of me."

I look at him and laugh. He can really ruin a romantic moment! Patch slaps the back of Bash's head and they both laugh.

We shower, eat ice cream, and discuss the magic of what just happened. All in all, we want to do it again soon. We snuggle into bed, me in the middle, and quickly drift to sleep.

CHAPTER TWENTY

It's early when I feel Patch slip out of bed. Instead of using the master bathroom, he leaves the bedroom and closes the door behind him. I turn my head and see Bash asleep with the blankets at rest about his waist. His hand holds his cock the same way Patch does as if to protect the most valued part of their bodies from danger while they sleep.

I slide close enough to trail my fingers down his arm. He scratches the spot. I tickle again and he scratches harder. His eyes open with a growling expression until he sees me lying next to him, watching him.

"Hello, handsome," I say, then repeat the tickle.

He reaches for my hand and lays it on his chest. "Good morning. Since when does Miss Sleepyhead wake before me?" I shrug. He says, "I could get used to it."

"It's a one-time thing so don't rely on me to get you up in time to go to work unless you enjoy being late."

Bash lifts his head to look over me at the empty spot. "Patch gone to his room?"

"He just left. I'm not sure where he went, but I assume so." I roll toward him and kiss his chest. "Last one up is a rotten egg." He jerks and I leap off the bed only to realize how achy my body is.

He snickers. "Ropes are a bitch, aren't they?"

"I don't think it was the ropes themselves so much as how hard I fought against them." I wave my eyebrows. "I'm beginning to think being bound is my guilty pleasure."

After a few stretches, I toss on a purple nightgown with a cartoon bear on the front and head to the bathroom to freshen up before I go to the kitchen.

"Hello, beautiful," Patch says as my feet slap the cool wood floor with each step. He waits for a kiss before he hands me the mug of coffee he readied for me.

"Thank you," I say with a smile. I groan. "I'm so sore today. You guys really gave it to me last night."

He stops taking things out of the freezer to look at me. "If you're rather us take it easy on you from now on—"

"Ha!" I yelp. "Hell, no!" I sip the liquid of the gods. "Totally worth every ache and pain."

"I'll have you know my knee is giving me shit today," he says as he swings his right calf and grumbles.

"Hey, I was thinking," I say just before Bash walks in the kitchen.

"Good morning, brother!" Bash says and takes a mug from the cupboard, then heads toward the coffee pot. "Yes! Mm, breakfast!"

"As I was saying," I continue. "We should pack up the ingredients and bring everything to the main house."

They both agree but Patch says, "We can check in on the lovely couple to see how their evening went."

After we shower and dress, we pack everything in a cooler and climb into my car. I sit in the back to let the boys chat. Bash zips down the driveway and speeds down the highway that leads to the driveway of the main house. He stops so Patch can collect the mail from the flag risen box.

He reaches for the handle but Bash jerks the car forward a few feet. Patch scowls as he reaches for it again. Bash jerks the car forward just enough that he has to reach further. Patch whips open the door then drops into the car and throws his body weight against Bash and pins him to the door.

Bash grunts breathlessly and can only manage to whisper. "Get the fuck off me, cow!" They both laugh like brothers do all the way to the main house.

We walk in and expect them to be awake but it's quiet. Mack's bedroom door is slightly ajar so I slowly push it open.

The sliver of sunlight seeping through the gap in the drapes does not reveal a sleeping Mack.

Lizzy's straddled over his face with a strong grip on the wooden headboard. I can see Mack's chin move beneath her as she slowly sways her hips. Her red hair flows down her pale shoulders with messy disregard. She's shockingly beautiful and she nears orgasm. Her ribs widen her back as she sucks in her breaths.

Her head whips around and her eyes dart to mine. I should retreat from the room but when she doesn't startle, my feet seem to cement themselves to the floor. I can't look away, neither can she. Her whimpers are like soft, sexy music. She moans and her eyelids droop. Her chin drops to her chest as her body quivers. She gasps and pants before her shoulders slump forward.

She shivers then lifts off his face. Her hair blocks me from seeing their kiss. I should walk away and close the door. I should. Why can't I leave?

Lizzy whispers something to Mack before she stands. He looks at me and grins. "Are you next?" He reaches his hand out to me and waves his fingers to urge me to go to him.

I snicker while I lean against the doorframe and cross my arms over my chest. "I don't think I could if I wanted to." They both look at me as if waiting for me to continue. "Patch bound me in rope and they dual fucked me. I'm exhausted and every muscle in my body aches."

Lizzy pulls a black t-shirt over her head and rams her arms in, pulling the snug fit shirt over her perky tits. "You're a lucky girl!" She slips her legs in her panties. "That's something I've always wanted to do—two guys at once."

"Put it on your bucket list," I say with a grin.

She laughs and pulls on a pair of yoga pants. She fluffs her tangled hair as she crosses the room toward me and a naked Mack sits on the edge of the bed.

She whispers, "He is really good at that." I nod and she kisses me as friends do. "Are you okay?" Again, I nod but this time my lip is pinched between my teeth. She smiles and winks as she leaves the room.

I remain to make sure Mack is able to manage his pajama pants. He asks, "Are you okay with what you saw?" He stands and pulls them up.

I nod. "Yeah! Absolutely." He stands and we take a few steps toward each other. "That was," pause in search of the words, "fucking beautiful. I hadn't expected to see that, but I'm glad I did."

He tilts his head and brushes a stray lock of hair behind my ear. "Why is that?"

"Because of how I feel about it. It's confirmation that I like her being with you guys. I'm not jealous at all. I'm no longer nervous about her being with Bash, should that situation arise." He kisses me and I can smell her on his face. I crinkle my nose. "Um, you should wash your face." He smiles apologetically and I shrug as I turn to walk out of his bedroom. "It's okay, I didn't hate it."

Lizzy has to leave almost right away. Her shift at the hospital starts in less than an hour from now and she still needs to get home to shower and change.

The guys and I eat and talk about what we all did the night before. Mack tells us that she came in through the night to ask if he needed anything. He said he didn't say anything, he just looked up and down her body. She stripped, and it went from there.

He said he felt useless since he can't move around very much. She rode him slowly because the pain from his bruised ribs was too unbearable when she bucked hard.

Mack likes her. Patch likes her. I'm sure Bash will, too.

***

Bash and Patch had to work this morning so I stayed to help Mack; who can mostly care for himself other than bathing and tasks that require two hands.

I love my time alone with Mack. He's very sweet, funny, and he loves to talk, so I don't have to hold up the conversation. After I've prepared his lunch, he insists he'll be fine alone. I try to argue but he's persistent.

The walk home through the woods is peaceful and quiet aside from the sounds of the forest. The smell of moss tickles my nostrils and I savor it. Nothing reminds me more of my happy childhood more than the smell of damp moss.

At two o'clock, Mack calls me and sounds distressed. "Goldie, are you busy?"

I set my book down and sense something's wrong. "Are you okay?"

He grumbles. "I'm fine, but I could use some help."

I walk into the house and set my book on the end table. "What's the matter?"

As I sling my purse strap over my shoulder he explains. "Well, I tried to make a coffee and dropped the container."

"Oh, shit! Let me guess," I say while I walk to my car. "Coffee grounds are all over the floor."

"Ah, well," he pauses and I can picture him peering down at the floor and shrugging his healthy shoulder. "There's a lot going on over here."

"I'm in the car. I'll be there in a few minutes. Go sit down somewhere and try not to make more of a mess." I laugh as I hang up.

I walk into the house and toss my purse on the table by the door and stride toward the kitchen. "Where's the mess? Mack?" I make my way around the island and look at the floor expecting a mess. "Mack, where did you drop the coffee? Did you already clean…" My words catch in my throat and I can't believe my eyes.

All three men are dressed in tuxedos. Patch and Mack are side by side, each holding a dozen red roses. Mack's jacket is draped over his casted arm. Bash is down on one knee and a single white rose lies beside his foot. He holds a small open box.

Patch waves me over and it's what I needed to snap me out of my trance. My feet weigh a ton and yet I think I hover above the floor. I stand before Bash and take a breath. I think it's my first one since I noticed them.

Bash swallows. "Goldilocks, I've loved you since the day I walked into that classroom a shy little boy. Our eyes met and you smiled at me. My tummy felt funny; nauseous but in a good way. I didn't know it then, but as we aged my desire to be yours never wavered even though I doubted the probability of our union. And now, as you stand before me… before us," he pauses to swallow.

His voice cracks. "It's been a lifetime in the making. I kneel before you, as vulnerable as that little boy who first met your eyes." He fights back tears. "I want to fall in love with you every single day." He blinks and tears spill. "Will you marry me?"

I'm a blubbering mess and can barely speak when he plucks the ring from the box and holds it before me, hoping I'll slip my finger into it. "Yes, of course, I'll marry you."

I lift my hand and spread my fingers. The ring is a perfect fit and absolutely gorgeous.

He stands, holding my cheeks in his palms, and kisses me three times before he hugs me. Patch taps Bash and he steps back but continues to hold my newly ringed hand.

Patch hands me the roses before he kisses me. "Congratulations, Goldilocks." He grabs Bash's shoulder and pulls him into a hug and mumbles something into his tuxedo-clad shoulder.

Mack kisses me softly, then brushes his thumb on my chin as his eyes shine with tears. "Welcome to the family." He places his roses over my arm atop Patch's. He wraps his arms around Bash and they hug while I blink and try to see the ring through the pools of tears.

The setting is small. It contains two small pearls that rest on either side of a much larger pearl. They're off-white and set on a silver band. It's beautiful, small and showy. It's perfectly suited for my personality.

"It was our mother's ring," Bash says as he takes my hand, allowing my fingers to drape between his thumb and forefinger. They all stare at it as if seeing it on my finger brings back happier memories of their mother. "She would have loved to know you and I are together, and she'd want you to have it."

Patch cuts in. "Bash wanted to add to it to include Mack and me."

Mack cuts him off. "The little pearls represent us."

Bash clears his throat rather loudly and they take a step back. "Patch and Mack love you, too. Although you'll be saying yes to me, they'll always be—I mean, they'll be there—"

I interrupt him. "I know what the ring represents to you," I pause to look at Patch and Mack then back at Bash. "To all of you. I'm not just giving myself and my heart to you, Bash." My smile grows. "You come as a package deal. I know what I'm getting into."

With a smile plastered on his face, Bash asks, "So when do you want to do this thing?"

"First I have to ask Lizzy if she'll be my maid of honor."

The corners of Patch's mouth turn up. "We're sharing the role of best man so I guess that means…"

Mack thrusts his fist in the air. "Two-on-one sex at your wedding in the coat closet with the maid of honor!"

The End

Continue the story of Goldilocks, Patch, Mack, and Bash with
GOLDILOCKS AND THE THREE BEAR BROTHERS:
LIBERATED, Book Four.
https://books2read.com/Goldilocks-BookFour

ABOUT THE AUTHOR

Pebbles Lacasse is a contemporary romance and erotica author. She leans toward writing bad boys desiring women who didn't know they have a kinky side. However, she's also known for her women with a dominant nature, and a secret yearning to be loved. Her books and short stories often take her readers into the BDSM lifestyle while revolving around real-life issues, and there's always a happy ending. The captivating stories of romance, love, and tender moments keep her readers coming back for more.

As someone living with Porphyria, Pebbles stays indoors to avoid UV light which gives her plenty of time to write. That's not to say she doesn't love "glamping," fishing, kayaking, and swimming, she just has to do it with protective clothing. If there's something she wants to do, she'll find a way to make it happen.

Pebbles is very family oriented. She and her husband of 30+ years raised their children in southern Ontario where she was born, and remains to this day. A 150+ lbs Mastiff takes up a lot of room in their home and in their hearts. His best friends are the two rescue cats that think they rule the home. The chickens couldn't care less about the dog until he chases them when they come too close to his outdoor toys.

Discover more about Pebbles on her website
www.pebbleslacasse.com

Free short story with newsletter subscription:
https://bit.ly/pebbleskinkynews

<u>Keep swiping for more books you may enjoy!</u>

MORE BOOKS BY PEBBLES LACASSE

Full Novels & Series
My Wife and Master Jake
Broken Charm

The Complete My JoeSmith Collection Boxed Set:
    My JoeSmith: Anonymity, Book One
    My JoeSmith: Anonymity, Book Two
    My JoeSmith: Nurture, Book Three
    My JoeSmith: Unity, Book Four
The Coaching Rayna Two Book Series:
    Coaching Rayna, Book One
    Coaching Rayna: Bound Hearts, Book Two
The Naughty Goldie Series:
    Goldilocks & The Three Bear Brothers, Book One
    Goldilocks & The Three Bear Brothers: Trifecta, Book Two
    Goldilocks & The Three Bear Brothers: Overture, Book Three
    Goldilocks & The Three Bear Brothers, Book Four
Rule Breakers: My Best Friend's Brother, Book One

Short Stories
Little Miss Muffet
Hello Officer
Mistress Rabbit
A Run with Charley
Carter's Mistress
Still Waters Burn Deep
Dominatrix for Hire

Anthologies
Quarantined: A Boxed Set of Pandemic Proportions –
Still Waters Burn Deep

To read teasers and see book cover photoshoot photos by Pebbles, and so much more, visit www.PebblesLacasse.com

CONNECT WITH PEBBLES

Follow me on Amazon and the links below:

Facebook
https://www.facebook.com/PebblesLacasseEroticRomanceWrit
er/

Facebook Group
www.facebook.com/groups/pebbleslacasseandfriendsgroup/

Newsletter sign-up
https://bit.ly/pebbleskinkynews

Website
https://www.pebbleslacasse.com

Instagram
https://www.instagram.com/pebbleslacasse/

Twitter
https://twitter.com/pebbleslacasse

Goodreads
http://bit.ly/Goodreads_2y5xJji

Bookbub
https://www.bookbub.com/profile/pebbles-lacasse

Youtube
http://www.youtube.com/@pebbleslacasse7554

TikTok
https://shorturl.at/SOzO8

SUBSCRIBE TO PEBBLES' NEWSLETTER

Sign up to receive Pebbles Lacasse's newsletter and receive a free short story to welcome you. Be among the first to read teasers from the books she's writing, learn what Pebbles does to keep her busy when she isn't writing her steamy novels, discover the captivating authors she's reading, be led to books with similar genres grouped together just for readers like you, and other crazy antics.
https://bit.ly/pebbleskinkynews

JOIN PEBBLES' TEAM

Would you like to be a valued member of my ***ARC team***? Advanced Readers receive copies of my soon-to-be published novels to read with the promise to leave reviews by the date set by Pebbles.
*You'll get **my books for FREE** forever as long as you leave reviews!*

Sound like a good deal?
https://forms.gle/gseo39XRubENVWjA9